STORIES FOR
FUN AND ADVENTURE

Stories for
Fun and Adventure

A Collection for All Boys and Girls
Who Love Good Stories

Selected and with an introduction by
PHYLLIS FENNER and MARY McCREA

The John Day Company
New York

Library of Congress Catalogue Card Number: 61-11831

ACKNOWLEDGMENTS

The editors make acknowledgment as follows for
permission to reprint the stories in this volume: to
William Morrow and Company, Inc., for "Henry and
Ribs," from *Henry Huggins*, by Beverly Cleary, copyright 1950 by William Morrow and Company, Inc.;
to Children's Press, Inc., for "John Colter's Race for
Life," by Edith McCall, from *Heroes of Western Outposts*, and for "Six Foolish Fishermen," by Benjamin
Elkin; to Holiday House, for "Whitey and the Rustlers," by Glen Rounds; to Story Parade, Inc., for "A
Pound of Pluck," by Mark Hager, copyright 1952 by

To our fathers and mothers who
were our first teachers and inspired
us to investigate the world of books

P.F.

M.M.

Contents

Introduction   11

Henry and Ribs
   BY BEVERLY CLEARY   15

John Colter's Race for Life
   BY EDITH MCCALL   30

Whitey and the Rustlers
   BY GLEN ROUNDS   41

Six Foolish Fishermen
   BY BENJAMIN ELKIN   55

A Pound of Pluck
   BY MARK HAGER   60

Seven Spears
   BY RUTHERFORD MONTGOMERY   67

The Day the Cow Sneezed
   BY JAMES FLORA   74

The Bottom of the Batting List
   BY MARION RENICK   81

10 *Contents*

Henry's Dog Henry
BY WALTER R. BROOKS   95

Big Rig
BY BILL AND ROSALIE BROWN   104

The Long Road to Boston
BY ELIZABETH COATSWORTH   126

The Snake in the Bottle
BY RUSSELL DAVIS AND BRENT ASHABRANNER   140

Calico the Wonder Horse
BY VIRGINIA LEE BURTON   144

Mr. Dawson Flies a Kite
BY R. O. WORK   154

A Hero by Mistake
BY ANITA BRENNER   162

The Hundred Dresses
BY ELEANOR ESTES   172

INTRODUCTION

There were several children in the special reading group. "The bedraggled dog was a retriever," read Jimmy with a very peculiar and hesitant pronunciation of "bedraggled" and "retriever." "Oh, well," he said cheerfully when the teacher corrected him, "what difference does it make as long as you know that one means messed up and the other a dog?"

Occasional hard words do not spoil a story for the reader because he can grasp the meaning from the context, and that occasional word enlarges his vocabulary.

Anyone who has tried to find interesting material for the older child who is reading on a low level knows how discouraging it is for everyone concerned. Countless books have been written for the beginning reader of six years old, and most of these are geared to a word list of fifty words or more. "The forgotten man" is the boy or girl who is too old

11

Introduction

to be interested in the subject matter of the beginner books (more likely a boy, since boys form the bigger percentage of our reading problems). While many picture books have stories that might interest the older child, he wouldn't be caught dead looking at them, for in his mind they are baby books.

Having worked with this problem for years, and worried over it, we have chosen these stories and tested them with children of different ages, grades and abilities who were finding reading difficult. We learned not only that the children could read them, but that the stories stimulated their desire to read for fun and adventure. In many instances they wanted to finish the book from which the incident was taken or they wanted to read other stories by the same author.

These stories have been chosen with an eye on the older child and they have not been changed from the original in any way.

Some stories are very short, for as one boy said, "I like to read something that I don't have to stop in the middle of the chapter." It gives the reluctant reader a feeling of satisfaction to be able to finish something.

Several of the stories were published originally in picture-book format. However, the story without the pictures is of interest to any age.

Since we have found that these stories appeal to children of different ages, grades, and abilities, this book serves two purposes. It is a good anthology for the able or average younger reader and it is material for the older child who is having a hard time finding stories on his interest level that he can read.

P.F.
M.M.

STORIES FOR
FUN AND ADVENTURE

HENRY AND RIBS

BEVERLY CLEARY

Henry Huggins lived with his mother and father in a square white house on Klickitat Street. Except for having his tonsils out when he was six and breaking his arm falling out of a cherry tree when he was seven, nothing much happened to Henry.

I wish something exciting would happen, Henry often thought.

But nothing very interesting ever happened to

Henry, at least not until one Wednesday afternoon in March. Every Wednesday after school Henry rode downtown on the bus to go swimming at the Y.M.C.A. After he swam for an hour, he got on the bus again and rode home just in time for dinner. It was fun but not really exciting.

When Henry left the Y.M.C.A. on this particular Wednesday, he stopped to watch a man tear down a circus poster. Then, with three nickels and one dime in his pocket, he went to the corner drugstore to buy a chocolate ice cream cone. He thought he would eat the ice cream cone, get on the bus, drop his dime in the slot, and ride home.

That is not what happened.

He bought the ice cream cone and paid for it with one of his nickels. On his way out of the drugstore he stopped to look at funny books. It was a free look, because he had only two nickels left.

He stood there licking his chocolate ice cream cone and reading one of the funny books when he heard a thump, thump, thump. Henry turned, and there behind him was a dog. The dog was scratching himself. He wasn't any special kind of dog. He was too small to be a big dog but, on the other hand, he was much too big to be a little dog. He wasn't a white dog, because parts of him were brown and other parts were black and in between there were yellowish patches. His ears stood up and his tail was long and thin.

The dog was hungry. When Henry licked, he licked. When Henry swallowed, he swallowed.

"Hello, you old dog," Henry said. "You can't have my ice cream cone."

Swish, swish, swish went the tail. "Just one bite," the dog's brown eyes seemed to say.

"Go away," ordered Henry. He wasn't very firm about it. He patted the dog's head.

The tail wagged harder. Henry took one last lick. "Oh, all right," he said. "If you're that hungry, you might as well have it."

The ice cream cone disappeared in one gulp.

"Now go away," Henry told the dog. "I have to catch a bus for home."

The dog sat down at Henry's feet. Henry looked at the dog and the dog looked at Henry.

"I don't think you've got a home. You're awful thin. Your ribs show right through your skin."

Thump, thump, thump, replied the tail.

"And you haven't got a collar," said Henry.

He began to think. If only he could keep the dog! He had always wanted a dog of his very own and now he had found a dog that wanted him. He couldn't go home and leave a hungry dog on the street corner. If only he knew what his mother and father would say! He fingered the two nickels in the pocket. That was it! He would use one of the nickels to phone his mother.

"Come on, Ribsy. Come on, Ribs, old boy. I'm going to call you Ribsy because you're so thin."

The dog trotted after the boy to the telephone booth in the corner of the drugstore. Henry shoved him into the booth and shut the door. He had never used a pay telephone before. He had to put the telephone book on the floor and stand on tiptoe on it to reach the mouthpiece. He gave the operator his number and dropped his nickel into the coin box.

"Hello — Mom?"

"Why, Henry!" His mother sounded surprised. "Where are you?"

"At the drugstore near the Y."

Ribs began to scratch. Thump, thump, thump. Inside the telephone booth the thumps sounded loud and hollow.

"For goodness' sake, Henry, what's that noise?" his mother demanded. Ribs began to whimper and then to howl. "Henry," Mrs. Huggins shouted, "are you all right?"

"Yes, I'm all right," Henry shouted back. He never could understand why his mother always thought something had happened to him when nothing ever did. "That's just Ribsy."

"Ribsy?" His mother was exasperated. "Henry, will you please tell me what is going on?"

"I'm trying to," said Henry. Ribsy howled louder. People were gathering around the phone booth to see what was going on. "Mother, I've found a dog. I sure wish I could keep him. He's a good dog and I'd feed him and wash him and everything. Please, Mom."

"I don't know, dear," his mother said. "You'll have to ask your father."

"Mom!" Henry wailed. "That's what you always say!" Henry was tired of standing on tiptoe and the phone booth was getting warm. "Mom, please say yes and I'll never ask for another thing as long as I live!"

"Well, all right, Henry. I guess there isn't any reason why you shouldn't have a dog. But you'll have to bring him home on the bus. Your father has the car today and I can't come after you. Can you manage?"

"Sure! Easy."

"And Henry, please don't be late. It looks as if it might rain."

"All right, Mom." Thump, thump, thump.

"Henry, what's that thumping noise?"

"It's my dog Ribsy. He's scratching a flea."

"Oh, Henry," Mrs. Huggins moaned. "Couldn't you have found a dog without fleas?"

Henry thought that was a good time to hang up. "Come on, Ribs," he said. "We're going home on the bus."

When the big green bus stopped in front of the drugstore, Henry picked up his dog. Ribsy was heavier than he expected. He had a hard time getting into the bus and was wondering how he would get a dime out of his pocket when the driver said, "Say, sonny, you can't take that dog on the bus."

"Why not?" asked Henry.

"It's a company rule, sonny. No dogs on buses."

"Golly, Mister, how'm I going to get him home? I just have to get him home."

"Sorry, sonny. I didn't make the rule. No animal can ride on a bus unless it's inside a box."

"Well, thanks anyway," said Henry doubtfully, and lifted Ribsy off the bus.

"Well, I guess we'll have to get a box. I'll get you onto the next bus somehow," promised Henry.

He went back into the drugstore followed closely by Ribsy. "Have you got a big box I could have, please?" he asked the man at the toothpaste counter. "I need one big enough for my dog."

The clerk leaned over the counter to look at Ribsy. "A cardboard box?" he asked.

"Yes, please," said Henry, wishing the man would hurry. He didn't want to be late getting home.

The clerk pulled a box out from under the counter. "This hair tonic carton is the only one I have. I guess it's big enough, but why anyone would want to put a dog in a cardboard box I can't understand."

The box was about two feet square and six inches deep. On one end was printed, "Don't Let Them Call You Baldy," and on the other, "Try Our Large Economy Size."

Henry thanked the clerk, carried the box out to the bus stop, and put it on the sidewalk. Ribsy padded after him. "Get in, fellow," Henry commanded. Ribsy understood. He stepped into the box and sat down just as the bus came around the corner. Henry had to kneel to pick up the box. It was not a very strong box and he had to put his arms under it. He staggered as he lifted it, feeling like the strong man who lifted weights at the circus. Ribsy lovingly licked his face with his wet pink tongue.

"Hey, cut that out!" Henry ordered. "You better be good if you're going to ride on the bus with me."

The bus stopped at the curb. When it was Henry's turn to get on, he had trouble finding the step because he couldn't see his feet. He had to try several times before he hit it. Then he discovered he had forgotten to take his dime out of his pocket. He was afraid to put the box down for fear Ribsy might escape.

He turned sideways to the driver and asked politely, "Will you please take the dime out of my pocket for me? My hands are full."

The driver pushed his cap back on his head and exclaimed, "Full! I should say they are full! And just where do you think you're going with that animal?"

"Home," said Henry in a small voice.

The passengers were staring and most of them were smiling. The box was getting heavier every minute.

"Not on this bus, you're not!" said the driver.

"But the man on the last bus said I could take the dog on the bus in a box," protested Henry, who was afraid he couldn't hold the dog much longer. "He said it was a company rule."

"He meant a big box tied shut. A box with holes punched in it for the dog to breathe through."

Henry was horrified to hear Ribsy growl. "Shut up," he ordered.

Ribsy began to scratch his left ear with his left hind foot. The box began to tear. Ribsy jumped out of the box and off the bus and Henry jumped after him. The bus pulled away with a puff of exhaust.

"Now see what you've done! You've spoiled everything." The dog hung his head and tucked his tail between his legs. "If I can't get you home, how can I keep you?"

Henry sat down on the curb to think. It was so late and the clouds were so dark that he didn't want to waste time looking for a big box. His mother was probably beginning to worry about him.

People were stopping on the corner to wait for the next bus. Among them Henry noticed an elderly lady carrying a large paper shopping bag full of apples. The shopping bag gave him an idea. Jumping up, he snapped his fingers at Ribsy and ran back into the drugstore.

"You back again?" asked the toothpaste clerk.

"What do you want this time? String and paper to wrap your dog in?"

"No, sir," said Henry. "I want one of those big nickel shopping bags." He laid his last nickel on the counter.

"Well, I'll be darned," said the clerk, and handed the bag across the counter.

Henry opened the bag and set it up on the floor. He picked up Ribsy and shoved him hind feet first into the bag. Then he pushed his front feet in. A lot of Ribsy was left over.

The clerk was leaning over the counter watching. "I guess I'll have to have some string and paper, too," Henry said, "if I can have some free."

"Well! Now I've seen everything." The clerk shook his head as he handed a piece of string and a big sheet of paper across the counter.

Ribsy whimpered, but he held still while Henry wrapped the paper loosely around his head and shoulders and tied it with a string. The dog made a lumpy package, but by taking one handle of the bag in each hand Henry was able to carry it to the bus stop. He didn't think the bus driver would notice him. It was getting dark and a crowd of people, most of them with packages, was waiting on the corner. A few spatters of rain hit the pavement.

This time Henry remembered his dime. Both hands were full, so he held the dime in his teeth and stood behind the woman with the bag of apples. Ribsy wiggled and whined, even though Henry tried to pet him through the paper. When the bus stopped, he climbed on behind the lady, quickly set the bag down, dropped his dime in the slot, picked up the bag, and squirmed through the crowd to a seat beside a fat man near the back of the bus.

"Whew!" Henry sighed with relief. The driver was the same one he had met on the first bus! But Ribs was on the bus at last. Now if he could only keep him quiet for fifteen minutes they would be home and Ribsy would be his for keeps.

The next time the bus stopped Henry saw Scooter McCarthy, a fifth grader at school, get on and make his way through the crowd to the back of the bus.

Just my luck, thought Henry. I'll bet he wants to know what's in my bag.

"Hi," said Scooter.

"Hi," said Henry.

"Whatcha got in the bag?" asked Scooter.

"None of your beeswax," answered Henry.

Scooter looked at Henry. Henry looked at Scooter. Crackle, crackle, crackle went the bag. Henry tried to hold it more tightly between his knees.

"There's something alive in that bag," Scooter said accusingly.

"Shut up, Scooter!" whispered Henry.

"Aw, shut up yourself!" said Scooter. "You've got something alive in that bag."

By this time the passengers at the back of the bus were staring at Henry and his package. Crackle, crackle, crackle. Henry tried to pat Ribsy again through the paper. The bag crackled even louder. Then it began to wiggle.

"Come on, tell us what's in the bag," coaxed the fat man.

"N-n-n-nothing," stammered Henry. "Just something I found."

"Maybe it's a rabbit," suggested one passenger. "I think it's kicking."

"No, it's too big for a rabbit," said another.

"I'll bet it's a baby," said Scooter. "I'll bet you kidnaped a baby!"

"I did not!"

Ribs began to whimper and then to howl. Crackle, crackle, crackle. Thump, thump, thump. Ribsy scratched his way out of the bag.

"Well, I'll be doggoned!" exclaimed the fat man and began to laugh. "I'll be doggoned!"

"It's just a skinny old dog," said Scooter.

"He is not! He's a good dog."

Henry tried to keep Ribsy between his knees. The bus lurched around a corner and started to go uphill. Henry was thrown against the fat man. The frightened dog wiggled away from him, squirmed between the passengers, and started for the front of the bus.

"Here, Ribsy, old boy! Come back here," called Henry and started after him.

"E-e-ek! A dog!" squealed the lady with the bag of apples. "Go away, doggie, go away!"

Ribsy was scared. He tried to run and crashed into the lady's bag of apples. The bag tipped over and the apples began to roll toward the back of the bus, which was grinding up a steep hill. The apples rolled around the feet of the people who were standing. Passengers began to slip and slide. They dropped their packages and grabbed one another.

Crash! A high-school girl dropped an armload of books.

Rattle! Bang! Crash! A lady dropped a big paper bag. The bag broke open and pots and pans rolled out.

Thud! A man dropped a coil of garden hose. The hose unrolled and the passengers found it wound around their legs.

People were sitting on the floor. They were sitting on books and apples. They were even sitting on other people's laps. Some of them had their hats over their faces and their feet in the air.

Skree-e-etch! The driver threw on the brakes and turned around in his seat just as Henry made his way through the apples and books and pans and hose to catch Ribsy.

The driver pushed his cap back on his head. "O.K., sonny," he said to Henry. "Now you know why dogs aren't allowed on buses!"

"Yes, sir," said Henry in a small voice. "I'm sorry."

"You're sorry! A lot of good that does. Look at this bus! Look at those people!"

"I didn't mean to make any trouble," said Henry. "My mother said I could keep the dog if I could bring him home on the bus."

The fat man began to snicker. Then he chuckled. Then he laughed and then he roared. He laughed until tears streamed down his cheeks and all the other passengers were laughing too, even the man with the hose and the lady with the apples.

The driver didn't laugh. "Take that dog and get off the bus!" he ordered. Ribsy whimpered and tucked his tail between his legs.

The fat man stopped laughing. "See here, driver," he said, "you can't put that boy and his dog off in the rain."

"Well, he can't stay on the bus," snapped the driver.

Henry didn't know what he was going to do. He guessed he'd have to walk the rest of the way home. He wasn't sure he knew the way in the dark.

Just then a siren screamed. It grew louder and louder until it stopped right alongside the bus.

A policeman appeared in the entrance. "Is there a boy called Henry Huggins on this bus?" he asked.

"Oh boy, you're going to be arrested for having a dog on the bus!" gloated Scooter. "I'll bet you have to go to jail!"

"I'm him," said Henry in a very small voice.

"I am he," corrected the lady with the apples, who had been a schoolteacher and couldn't help correcting boys.

"You'd better come along with us," said the policeman.

"Boy, you're sure going to get it!" said Scooter.

"Surely going to get it," corrected the apple lady.

Henry and Ribsy followed the policeman off the bus and into the squad car, where Henry and the dog sat in the back seat.

"Are you going to arrest me?" Henry asked timidly.

"Well, I don't know. Do you think you ought to be arrested?"

"No, sir," said Henry politely. He thought the policeman was joking, but he wasn't sure. It was hard to tell about grownups sometimes. "I didn't mean to do anything. I just had to get Ribsy home. My mother said I could keep him if I could bring him home on the bus."

"What do you think?" the officer asked his partner, who was driving the squad car.

"We-e-ell, I think we might let him off this time," answered the driver. "His mother must be pretty wor-

ried about him if she called the police, and I don't
think she'd want him to go to jail."

"Yes, he's late for his dinner already. Let's see how
fast we can get him home."

The driver pushed a button and the siren began to
shriek. Ribsy raised his head and howled. The tires
sucked at the wet pavement and the windshield wip-
ers splip-splopped. Henry began to enjoy himself.
Wouldn't this be something to tell the kids at school!
Automobiles pulled over to the curb as the police car
went faster and faster. Even the bus Henry had been
on had to pull over and stop. Henry waved to the
passengers. They waved back. Up the hill the police
car sped and around the corner until they came to
Klickitat Street and then to Henry's block and then
pulled up in front of his house.

Henry's mother and father were standing on the
porch waiting for him. The neighbors were looking
out of their windows.

"Well!" said his father after the policeman had
gone. "It's about time you came home. So this is
Ribsy! I've heard about you, fellow, and there's a big
bone and a can of Feeley's Flea Flakes waiting for
you."

"Henry, what will you do next?" sighed his mother.

"Golly, Mom, I didn't do anything. I just brought
my dog home on the bus like you said."

Ribsy sat down and began to scratch.

JOHN COLTER'S
RACE FOR LIFE

EDITH McCALL

It took a hero to stay alive in the wilderness around
lonely outposts such as Fort Manuel. Sometimes even
the heroes took chances that were too big and fell.
But John Colter was one of the lucky ones who took
big chances and lived to tell his story.

He helped with the building of Fort Manuel. When
fall came, it was almost ready as a place to keep men
safe and as a center where the Indians would bring furs

to trade for the goods Mr. Manuel had brought from St. Louis. But someone had to spread the word that the trading post was there. John was chosen to be the messenger to go to the Indian tribes.

"You know your way in these mountains better than any other man," Mr. Manuel told him. "Carry the word to the Blackfoot Indians as well as the Crows. Tell them we will pay well for all furs they bring to Fort Manuel."

With a pack on his back, his gun and ammunition hung over his shoulder, and his tomahawk and knife in his belt, John set out alone to walk five hundred miles.

At night he cut evergreen boughs to make himself a shelter from the cold winds that swept through the mountain passes. All day he walked through the flame colored woods of the valleys. He saw many wild animals and shot what he needed for food, but no human being moved through the wilderness with him.

The wind was sweeping the tree limbs bare when he found the first tribes of Crow Indians in the upper valley of the Wind River. The Crows were gathering to meet their enemies, the Blackfeet, in war.

John had no choice. He had to fight with the Crows, when the Blackfeet came, or be killed. Before the battle was over, he had an arrow wound in his leg.

But worse than that, the Blackfeet Indians had seen him and marked him as an enemy.

John talked with the Crows about bringing their furs to Fort Manuel. Then he headed northeast toward the fort. He had given up further traveling until spring because of his wounded leg and because he knew the Blackfeet would try to kill him.

He walked through deep pine forests. One day he came out of the woods and found himself on the shore of a beautiful mountain lake. Near by he saw strange boiling springs with clouds of steam rising, not far from the coldest of mountain streams. He watched a great spurt of water rise high into the air. He had happened upon the wonders of what was to become Yellowstone National Park in Wyoming.

When he reached Fort Manuel, winter had set in. He told Mr. Manuel of all he had seen and of the battle between the Crows and the Blackfeet.

"I don't think the Blackfeet will do business with us," he said, rubbing his leg which still pained him.

But some of the men had met a few Blackfeet not far from the fort. "They seemed friendly enough, and interested in trading," Mr. Manuel told John. "In the spring, I would like you to try again, John. Go up to the three forks, where the Missouri River begins, to the heart of the Blackfoot country."

When John set out again in the early spring, two hunters went with him. The three men planned to trap beavers as they went up to the Blackfoot country. John led the way to the country just north and west of Yellowstone Park. They came one day to a fast running river.

"This is the first of the three rivers which meet to form the Missouri River," John told the other men. "Captain Lewis and Captain Clark named the three rivers after important men in our government. This first fork is the Gallatin. The middle river is the Madison, and the one farthest west is the Jefferson."

"Good beaver sign here," said one of the men, whose name was Potts. "We can trap our way to the headwaters of the Missouri."

The third man, Dixon, decided to trap this stream. Potts and Colter went on to the Jefferson. There they took time to cut down a tree from which to burn and chop out a small canoe. With it, they could paddle up the side streams to set traps.

John's leg was still bothering him. As he rubbed it one night he said, "Potts, every time this leg hurts, I remember the painted faces of those Blackfeet. I don't trust them at all, and I think we'd better be very careful from now on."

One morning, the two men were checking their traps in a small stream which ran into the Jefferson about six miles away. They were in the canoe, moving on to another trap when a sound from the bluffs alongside the stream made them look up.

"Blackfeet!" John said. "Let's get going!"

Potts had the paddle. At the sound of a horrible yell, he pushed for the nearest shore, thinking to run along the valley. But the yelling Indians came sliding down the bank. One of them reached into the canoe and grabbed Potts' rifle.

"Oh, no you don't!" cried John. He leaped ashore and took hold of the rifle at both ends. For a moment, Indian and white man faced each other, testing their strength. Then, with a mighty pull and a grunt, John broke the Indian's grip. He tossed the rifle back to Potts, who was still in the boat.

Potts was too frightened to think. He pushed the canoe out into the stream and began to paddle away. Before he had gone six feet, he screamed and pulled at an arrow in his shoulder.

"Come ashore!" yelled John. "They'd have killed us by now if they wanted to. We'll give ourselves up and see what happens."

But Potts raised his rifle and shot an Indian. As the man fell, a shower of arrows was aimed at Potts. The last John saw of him, he lay in the drifting boat, a dozen arrows in his back.

John turned to his captors. "All right. I'm your prisoner. What are you going to do with me?"

The Blackfeet pulled John to the top of the bluff and ripped off his clothing. From the little he had learned of their tongue, John understood some of them wanted to set him up as a shooting target. Others seemed to have some other idea.

An older man pushed his way up to John. "The chief," John decided. The braves let go of him as the chief spoke.

Then he turned to John and in sign language asked him, "Can you run fast?"

"What now?" John thought. If he said he could run fast — and he always had been able to outrun every boy and man he raced against — they would expect him to prove it against their best runners. He shook his head and said, "No."

The chief smiled. Then he gave an order to his braves.

"He's going to hold them back and give the poor, slow-running white man a head start," thought John. "So much the better. I'll need every break I can get if I'm to live through this."

The chief took John by the arm and led him about as far away from the waiting braves as one city block would be. All around him was the open plain. John was being given the chance to run for his life. Whoever caught him was to have the pleasure of killing him.

"Unh!" said the old chief, and gave John a little shove. John took off at a speed which surprised even himself. Behind him he heard the great war whoop which meant that all the braves who chose to do so were starting after him.

There was no time to pick his way. The open plain was dotted with clumps of a kind of cactus called "prickly pear." John felt the stabbing of its thorns in his bare feet before he had gone one hundred feet. He kept his eyes ahead on his only hope — the dark line, miles away, which marked the grove of cottonwood trees along the bank of the Jefferson River.

Pain was a part of his pounding feet. On and on he ran. He was almost halfway across the six-mile plain before he dared take time to look back over his shoulder. A quick look told him that the main body of Indians was far back, with a scattering of running braves ahead of it. But one Indian, a big fellow carrying a spear, was far ahead of the others. He ran with the stride of a giant, and John felt him gaining on him with each step. He was only about three hundred feet away.

"If I can get to the river — if only I can keep ahead of that one — " John's thoughts brought hope, and his pounding feet somehow went faster. In his chest he felt a pain as if his heart would leap out if it could. Suddenly his nose began to bleed. The warm blood ran down his face and onto his chest. John wasted no motion to try to stop it.

The dark line had grown much clearer, and the fringe of trees began to take form.

"About one more mile," John thought, and took a quick look to see where the big Indian was. What he saw told him that death was on his heels. The man was not more than sixty feet behind him.

A wild idea came into his head. Perhaps he could wrestle the man, and throw him for long enough to kill him with his own spear. All the other Indians seemed to have surrendered their prize to this one man. They were still coming, but more slowly.

His heart told him to keep on running — anything to get away from the man with a spear. His mind told him the spear would bring him down anyway, any second. Courage was all that could save him now.

Suddenly he stopped and wheeled about to face the oncoming Indian. He spread out his arms.

The Indian, only forty feet away, was taken by surprise. John's chest and face were red with blood. At the sight he tried to stop, raising his arm to throw the spear. The suddenness of it all made him trip. He fell, face down. The spear broke as it hit the ground and the Indian's hand held only a broken stick. The spearhead stuck into the ground near by.

John ran for the spearhead and pulled it from the ground. The Indian was trying to get up as John threw himself onto his back. The spearhead cut into the painted skin, and John felt the body grow still.

He felt faint. "I can't — " he thought, but the will to live is strong. In a moment, his tired legs were carrying him toward the river. He knew the other braves had seen what happened and would speed up again.

The cries behind him grew louder as, at last, he reached the cottonwood trees. He plunged on through and into the river.

His heart pounded as he felt the cool water about him. He rested only a moment and then looked for a hiding place.

"I'm in luck," he thought, and began to swim down the river towards an island. At the near end, driftwood had piled up. It floated in the river like an uneven sort of raft.

Drawing on his last bit of strength, John swam to the raft. He ducked under it and swam underwater until he saw a place where his head could be above water between some logs. Over the hole was a covering of smaller branches. He pushed his head and arms into the hole and pulled the small branches around him.

Then, at last, he could rest. His breath came in short, hoarse heaves.

Not three seconds more passed before John heard the first of the Indians rush through the cottonwood trees, screeching and yelling. John could see them searching the bank for signs of him. They followed his tracks to the water's edge. Some swam across and studied the bank on the far side for a long way. Others swam close to him as they headed for the island. Some even stepped onto the raft. John could have touched one with his hand.

"If only they don't set fire to this raft — or pull it apart for firewood," John thought, for he saw that some of the Indians had sat down on the island to rest. What if they should make camp there?

But about sunset all of them returned to the plain. John stayed in his hiding place until darkness had settled. Then, making no more sound than the feeding fish, he swam underwater the length of the island. He waited there a few minutes, listening. Then on he went, still swimming slowly and almost without sound.

When he was well below the island he took less care, but he went a long way down the Jefferson River before he at last climbed ashore. He did not want the Indians to find his tracks in the morning, and chose his spot carefully.

By this time, the chill of the mountain stream had gone through him. The night air was cold, too. Even if he had thought it safe to build a fire, he had nothing with which to do it. Each step on his thorn-ripped, stone-bruised feet was a flash of pain. Half walking, half crawling, he moved slowly in the direction of Fort Manuel.

It was a long, painful journey. John Colter had no clothes, no tools, no weapons, and no food but what his fingers could pull from the earth. The sun of the day burned him. The thin, cold mountain air of night was almost more than he could stand. He had to be always on the watch for Indians, grizzly bears or the gray wolf.

After several days, Fort Manuel was before him at last. He stumbled to the gate. The men found him there, more dead than alive.

When he could talk, John told his story. Mr. Manuel listened, able to believe it only because he saw the living man before him.

There was no further thought of going into Black-foot country. Mr. Manuel headed downriver to take the furs the Crow Indians had brought to the market at St. Louis. John Colter stayed on at the fort, building his strength and trapping in the near-by streams. He did not return to St. Louis until 1810, six years after he had left it to go on the great exploring trip with Lewis and Clark. He went to Captain Clark then, with much to tell him that added to the map of the Louisiana Territory.

Few people believed the story he told. They shook their heads and said, "Man couldn't possibly fight for his life like that!"

But John Colter wasn't an ordinary man. He was a hero.

WHITEY AND THE RUSTLERS

GLEN ROUNDS

It was a fine spring morning in Lone Tree County, with the prairie beginning to turn green, and the wild chokecherry and plum thickets smelling sweet. Magpies and meadow larks were talking big about the business of starting new nests.

Whitey was headed for Cedar Spring to see if the

windmill was working, but along the way he was looking for his two beef steers, which he ran with Uncle
Torwal's cattle. He hadn't noticed them around for
several days, and was a little worried.

Old Spot jogged along at his special ambling trot
and thought about the days when he'd been a first-
class cow horse. Whitey sat up straight and thought
about the fine new saddle he'd buy in the fall when
he sold those two steers of his.

He didn't really mind wearing a hand-me-down
Stetson of Uncle Torwal's, especially when it had such
a fine rattlesnake hatband, for most all cowboys wore
battered old hats. And for the same reason he didn't
mind the old boots with the run-over heels and the
fancy butterfly stitching on the tops, that he'd been
given by a puncher with small feet when he got a new
pair of Fort Worths.

But his old saddle was something else again. It was
an old Cogshell with a flat Texas horn. It was so old
the corners of the skirts were curled up tight, and the
strings had long ago been chewed off by calves. Everywhere the stitching was coming undone, leaving great
corners of old leather ticking up to give the whole
affair the look of a moulting hen. Furthermore, the
stirrups were the clumsy iron kind, when the style
hereabouts was a neat wooden oxbow pattern. For a
long time, Whitey had felt that the saddle spoiled his

whole appearance, making him look more like a homesteader than a cowboy.

Of course, when he'd been smaller and first come to live with Uncle Torwal and help him run the Lone Tree Ranch, it hadn't mattered so much. But now that he was getting on to ten years old and practically a top hand he had to think more about the appearance of his equipment. People set a lot of store by such things.

So last summer Uncle Torwal had given him two Whiteface calves. Together they figured out a brand for him, and sent it off to be registered after they'd put it on the calves with a running iron. It was a fine big squiggle on the ribs with three dots at the end.

The Rattlesnake brand, they called it. Whitey figured it was about as fine a brand as he knew of. He saw no reason why it shouldn't someday be as famous as the old "101." And Rattlesnake Ranch sounded good no matter how you said it!

So he rode on for a while, thinking about the time when the Rattlesnake brand would be on thousands of head of good beef cattle instead of only two, and he'd be able to have a new saddle every week if he felt like it. But just when he had started thinking about how fine a Sunday saddle would look, decorated with silver in the Mexican fashion, he came on a calf bogged in the mud around an old water hole, so he had to stop thinking about saddles for a while.

The old cow near by was in a nasty humor, bawling and swinging her tail, so he didn't feel it was safe to get down off Spot. That meant he'd have to rope the calf and drag it out. And as calves will do, that one had gotten out into the middle of the softest patch of gumbo, so that if Whitey missed his first cast, as he most usually did, he was bound to get his rope all muddy. That never did any throw rope any good, and was especially bad for a brand-new one like Whitey was carrying. He finally urged old Spot out onto the mud until he could reach down and drop the loop square on the calf.

After that he took a hitch around the saddle horn and in no time at all dragged the calf out onto solid ground. After he'd shaken the loop loose and the cow and calf had gone he found his rope was muddy after all, so he had to get off and find some dry grass to clean it with.

It was then he noticed the fuss a bunch of magpies were making in a little gully not far off, and decided to go see what it was they were doing. The rain the day before had washed deeply into a pile of dirt that had caved off the cutbank, exposing some corners of what looked to be green cowhides, fresh enough to attract the magpies.

After some tugging and digging, Whitey uncovered

three hides, which had apparently been carelessly buried by caving part of the bank onto them. Two hides carried his Rattlesnake brand, and the other Uncle Torwal's Lone Tree!

He sat down on the bank, and if he hadn't been almost a man grown he'd have bawled like a kid, for there went his hopes of a new saddle. The two Rattle-snake steers he'd counted on so much were now in some rustler's truck on the road to a butcher shop far off. He knew how the rustlers operated, going out at night with a truck and butchering two or three steers quickly, destroying the hides to prevent identification, and leaving to sell the meat before anyone knew they were about.

There'd been talk for some time that they must be operating around here, for ranchers all up and down the valley had been missing beef, but until now there hadn't been any kind of proof.

When Whitey rode into the ranch and up to the horse trough Torwal saw he looked mighty glum, but didn't say anything.

"Truck rustlers been getting our cattle," Whitey said as Spot was drinking.

"There's been talk of such," Torwal said. "But nobody knows for sure that I know of."

"I found three fresh hides over by Cedar Spring this morning," Whitey said. "They was buried in a washout." He brushed dust off his hat and waited for

Uncle Torwal to ask him some more. He was trying his best to talk as any cowboy would, instead of getting excited like a kid.

Torwal saw there must be more to the story, because three beef steers missing shouldn't make Whitey look so upset. So he said, casual like, "Was the brands cut out?" For usually the rustlers cut the brand out and burn it before burying the hide.

"Reckon they must have been careless this time," Whitey said. "One was a Lone Tree steer and the other two were Rattlesnake brand."

"Got both yours, did they?" Torwal said, and whistled. "That was tough goin', cleanin' out your whole spread."

"Yeah, that's a fact," Whitey said. "Looks like I'll ride this old hull a while longer." And he let Spot into the stable so Uncle Torwal wouldn't see how badly he really did feel.

They didn't say much as they cooked and ate dinner, but afterwards, as they sat on the porch, Torwal spoke up. "Reckon we might as well ride in and see the sheriff," he said. "Now that we know for sure that rustlers are working around here, maybe we can figure out something."

"I sure hope so," Whitey said. "They did me out of a new saddle and I wish I was old enough to swear!"

When they got to town they tied their horses and walked into the sheriff's office. Mr. Hairpants Hagadorn, the sheriff, shook hands with them while Mr. Fort Worth Wilkerson, the deputy sheriff, dragged out chairs.

After some polite talk of this and that, Torwal told the sheriff what Whitey had found.

"Was them hides fresh, son?" the sheriff asked Whitey.

"Yessir, they looked to be only a day or two there," Whitey told him.

"This is the first time we've had any proof," the sheriff said, "but there's been a lot of complaints of missin' beef critturs all up and down the valley."

"How you reckon they get in and out of the valley without anyone knowing?" Torwal wondered after a little.

"I been considering that myself," the sheriff told him. "They have to come through here or through Hill City to get in or out, and we've been watchin' both places close, yet nobody has seen any strangers or strange trucks."

"I wish we could catch them," Whitey spoke up. "I was goin' to get a new saddle with the money from the steers they got of mine!"

"Well, maybe you can figure how to catch them and use your share of the reward money for that saddle," the sheriff told him.

At the mention of REWARD, Whitey stopped looking at the posters and notices tacked over the sheriff's desk and brightened right up. "You mean there's a reward for those rustlers?" he asked.

"Sure," the sheriff told him. "I got the notice around here somewhere."

After some more talk they shook hands with the sheriff, the deputy sheriff, and a man who had wandered into the office looking for a place to sit down, and rode off towards the ranch.

As they rode along Whitey thought about that reward, and tried to figure out some way he could earn it. It seemed to him that getting a new saddle by trapping rustlers was even better than getting it by selling cattle.

"Uncle Torwal!" he said, suddenly remembering something. "A time or two lately I've noticed tracks of a truck or car up in that little limestone canyon the other side of Cedar Spring. I just figured it was somebody building fence, but it might be where those rustlers are getting into the canyon, do you suppose?"

Torwal thought a while. "It could be, maybe," he said. "There used to be an old road through there that went down into the Boxelder road. Maybe we might as well drop by and take a look at things up there."

They found that the old trail, which had for years been overgrown and washed out in places, did not show signs of use. The worst holes had been filled, and while it was still not a road one would drive for pleasure, it was plain that a truck could travel over it.

"Looks like this might be it, all right," Torwal allowed. "This trail comes out on the Boxelder road, where nobody would think of watching for them."

"Why don't we lay for them when they come back?" Whitey asked, thinking of the reward and his new saddle.

"Well," said Torwal, "they might not come back. Those dudes are pretty smart and don't often work the same place twice. That's why they are so hard to catch." After seeing how Whitey's face fell, he went on, "On the other hand, with a trick road like this they might feel safe for a while longer. From all the talk of missing cattle in the valley, they must have made several trips already."

"Tell you what," Torwal said after they'd started home. "We might take turns watching that canyon evenings for a while, just in case they did come back."

"Yessir!" Whitey agreed. "We'll catch 'em coming in and collect the rewards!"

"We don't want to bother them comin' in," Torwal corrected him. "We jest want to know when they come in so we'll have time to call the sheriff and catch them going out with the meat in the trucks for evidence."

Whitey still favored capturing the rustlers without interference from the sheriff, but he said nothing about it. He was bound he'd get that saddle the rustlers had done him out of, and even part of the reward would be enough.

"I'll take my blankets and go out right away to watch for them," he said.

"You won't need any blankets," Torwal told him. "Those fellers usually figure to come in just about sundown so they'll be able to locate the critturs they want before the dusk is gone. So if they aren't in sight by full dark they'll probably not come."

After Whitey had eaten an early supper and was leaving to watch the canyon, Uncle Torwal spoke up. "If they don't show up tonight, we'll take turns with the neighbors for a few nights."

"I don't want anyone to take turns," Whitey hollered. "I'm the one they cleaned out, and I'll watch every night!"

So every night for almost a week Whitey rode out to a small butte where he could watch the canyon. Every night he carefully hid Spot in a plum thicket and then crawled Indian fashion to the top of the butte, where he lay hidden in the sage brush like some oldtime scout. But nothing happened, and he was beginning to believe the rustlers had deserted the valley.

On the seventh night, he'd just started down to go home when he thought he heard a truck motor. He hurried back up the hill and the sound was plain there. It was a powerful motor, and working hard. Soon he could see the dimmed lights as they moved cautiously to the mouth of the canyon, where they were switched off and the motor stopped.

It was rustlers, sure enough!

Whitey had been complaining to himself because Uncle Torwal wouldn't let him bring his rifle and capture the rustlers single-handed, but tonight he thought of nothing but getting back to the ranch as soon as possible to tell Uncle Torwal and get word to the sheriff. It seemed to him then that it was really the sheriff's business to deal with such people.

Spot got the surprise of his life when Whitey clapped spurs and quirt onto him! He couldn't remember the last time he'd traveled faster than a trot. But as this seemed to be in the nature of a special occasion he did his best, and before long Whitey and Torwal were sitting out by the road waiting for the sheriff and his deputies to come by and pick them up. The word had spread, and by the time the sheriff got there, ranchers and cowboys from up and down the valley had gathered. Most of them carried rifles on their saddles, or pistols in their belts. Rustlers were not popular thereabouts, and Whitey was looking forward to a right exciting time when they caught up with them.

When the sheriff came they all went along to Cedar Spring and the little canyon. Whitey had been afraid someone would think to tell him to stay behind, but no one did, so he rode along.

The men had all been concealed in the plum thickets

for what seemed a mighty long time to Whitey, when
they heard the truck coming back.

"This is when the bullets start to fly!" Whitey thought,
as the sheriff stepped out into the light of the truck and
held up his hand. But the truck stopped without pro-
test. Deputies and ranch men flashed on flashlights
and swarmed all round it. Four weaselly-looking men
climbed carefully out and stood with their hands
raised while they and the truck were searched.

"There's plenty beef in here!" a deputy hollered.

"All right!" the sheriff answered. "One of you drive
the truck along behind me, and we'll haul these gents
down to our jail for a spell."

The rustlers didn't say anything, except to sort of
mutter to themselves. They didn't look like the tough
guys Whitey had been picturing in his mind. They
weren't wearing gun belts, and they didn't talk tough
to the sheriff. Worst of all, they wore bib overalls, like
farmers, and one even had on a straw hat and plow
shoes! Whitey was mighty disappointed in them.

Early next morning Whitey and Uncle Torwal went
to town, and Mr. Bugeye Beasly, editor of the *Lone
Tree Eagle*, interviewed Whitey.

The reward turned out to be only fifty dollars, and
that divided six ways, so there was not enough to buy
the saddle with. Whitey had built his hopes so high
on that reward, that he felt mighty bad for a few days.
But after reading what Mr. Beasly wrote about him

in the paper, how his alertness had helped make Lone Tree County free of rustlers and the like, he sort of got used to the idea of getting along with the old saddle another year.

Then one morning Torwal told him, "We gotta go to town this morning, Bub. Sheriff said something about wantin' t' see you."

All the way into town Whitey wondered what the sheriff could want. Maybe he wanted to make him a deputy or something. He imagined this and that, but never thought of the real answer. For after some talk the sheriff pointed to something tied up in a grain sack on the floor and told Whitey, "Feller left that here an' told me to give it to you."

Whitey opened it up and inside was a brand-new saddle, the decorations hand tooled, and the whang-leather tie strings shining bright yellow, the sheep-skin lining bright and clean, and the whole thing smelling of neat's foot oil and new leather. It was the most beautiful saddle Whitey had ever seen. On the back of the cantle was a small silver plate he'd missed at first. It was engraved:

TO WHITEY

FOR SERVICE IN RIDDING

LONE TREE COUNTY OF RUSTLERS

FROM THE LONE TREE STOCKMAN'S

ASS'N.

Whitey couldn't think of anything to say, so he just grinned and carried the saddle out to try how it looked on Spot.

SIX FOOLISH FISHERMEN

BENJAMIN ELKIN

Once there were six brothers who decided to go fishing. So they went to the river and picked good spots
from which to fish.

"I will sit in this boat," said the first brother.

"And I will kneel on this raft," said the second
brother.

"And I will lean on this log," said the third brother.

"And I will stand on this bridge," said the fourth brother.

"And I will lie on this rock," said the fifth brother.

"And I will walk on this bank," said the sixth brother.

And that is exactly what they did.

Each brother fished from the spot he had chosen, and each one had good luck.

But when it was time to go home, the brothers became a little worried.

"We have been near the river, and over the river, and on the river," said the brother in the boat. "One of us might easily have fallen into the water and been drowned. I shall count all the brothers to be sure there are six of us."

And he began to count: "I see one brother on the raft. That's *one*. And another on the log. That's *two*. And another on the bridge. That's *three*. And another on the rock. That's *four*. And another on the bank. That's *five*. Only *five!* Woe is me. We have lost a brother!" In his sorrow he didn't even notice that he had forgotten to count himself.

"Can it really be?" cried the brother on the raft. "Has one of us been drowned, and have we really lost a brother?"

And he, too, began to count: "I see one brother on the log. That's *one*. And another on the bridge. That's *two*. And another on the rock. That's *three*. And another on the bank. That's *four*. And another in the boat. That's *five*."

"Only *five*. What will our dear mother say?"

And he, too, didn't even notice that he had forgotten to count himself.

"Let me check from here!" cried the brother on the log.

"I see one brother on the bridge. That's *one*. And another on the rock. That's *two*. And another on the bank. That's *three*. And another in the boat. That's *four*. And another on the raft. That's *five*. *Five* in all, oh, unhappy day! Why did we ever come here, for one of us to be drowned!"

Then the fourth brother counted, and the fifth and the sixth— each one counted only five brothers because each forgot to include himself.

All the brothers went back to the shore and rushed sadly up and down the river's edge, trying to see the body of their poor drowned brother.

Then along came a boy who had also been fishing but who had not caught a single fish.

"What's the matter?" he asked. "You seem to have plenty of fish. Why do you all look so sad?"

"Because six of us came here to fish, and now there are only five of us left. One of our dear brothers has been drowned!"

The boy looked puzzled. "What do you mean, only five left? How do you figure that?"

"Look, I'll show you," said the eldest brother, and he pointed to his brothers:

One.

Two.

Three.

Four.

Five.

"Six of us came here, and now only five are going back. Sad is the day!"

The boy turned to hide his smile, and then he turned back. "I think I can help you find your lost brother," he said. "When I squeeze your hand, I want you to count."

As hard as he could, he squeezed the hand of each of the brothers, in turn.

"*One!*" yelled the first brother, and he rubbed his aching hand.

"*Two!*" cried the second brother, and he jumped up and down because of the hard squeeze.

"*Three!*" shouted the third brother.

"*Four!*" shrieked the fourth brother.

"*Five!*" screamed the fifth brother.

"*Six!*" roared the sixth brother.

SIX! The brothers looked at each other in delight.

There were six of them again!

They cheered for joy, and slapped each other on the back.

Gratefully, they turned to the boy. "Here," they said,

"we insist that you take all of our fish. We can never thank you enough for finding our dear, lost brother."

As the boy happily accepted their gift, the six foolish fishermen went their merry way.

A POUND OF PLUCK

MARK HAGER

The chickens squalled, and Banty crowed, and that was the sign of death in our chicken lot. Anxiously I broke into a run. I had to get there ahead of the folks who were coming with brooms, rocks, and sticks to kill my little fighting bantam rooster.

I had always taken the little rooster's part, but this time I couldn't say anything. There was the fresh-killed young rooster, and blood and the fighting bantam's feathers on the inch of fresh snow in the chicken lot.

Besides, Banty himself was bloody and reeling, and the very fact that he had crowed meant he'd fought and killed again, for the little rooster liked to crow after he'd won a hard fight. But his crowing only made the folks hate him more, and this dead chicken made five in all.

The folks said he couldn't stay any longer at our house. He had to go, and they looked at me.

"I'll sell him," I said. "I'll take him down to Mr. Honaker's store and sell him...."

I started with Banty on my shoulder, but a few steps down the road I stopped. Banty was trying to tell me about this fight. He would look up in my face with his head turned flat so he could see better with one eye, and try to tell me. I felt Banty's spurs where I'd filed them so he could protect himself against the roosters seven times his weight, but now I was sick. I'd made a killer out of Banty.

I stood and considered a while. I took the little rooster in my hands and guessed at his weight. "Can't weigh much over a pound," I said, and then I could see Mr. Honaker down at the store. He'd lay Banty on the scales, and then grin at me and say, "Thirty cents..."

The thought of it made me want to cry. I didn't think it was fair to sell some things by the pound —

things like spunk and pluck and grit and fighting hearts.

I was looking down and about to cry, when I saw the mink tracks. A mink had crossed the road toward the creek. The tracks were coming from our chicken lot.

I stood still a minute and shivered. Banty was still trying to mutter something to me about his fight, and now I felt I knew a little bit about Banty's last fight, for I saw the mink was dropping blood now and then in the snow.

I pitched Banty back in the chicken lot and slipped in the house and got my twenty-two rifle. As I ran back past the chicken lot, I called to the little rooster. I tried to tell him it was my turn to fight for him, and I wished I could make him understand.

I went down the creek on the trail of the mink. For half a mile down the creek I trailed it, and once I found where the mink had stopped in the snow. It had circled and backtracked, as if hesitating which way from there.

Then I got lined out on the trail again, and I could tell the mink was making a wide circle. It left the creek and climbed a steep ridge, and from the ridge-top it circled toward our chicken lot again. I tried to break into a run on the trail, but a sudden peppering down of snow dimmed it, and soon I could not follow. But I wondered, could this mink with the taste of Banty's blood be heading back for the kill?

Though I couldn't follow the trail any more, I was pretty sure now of the mink's intentions. It had got madder and madder, and decided not to retreat any more but return to the chicken lot for the unfinished fight.

As I ran, I thought of the little rooster. I thought of his spunk and it made me sick. Banty could fly like a hawk, and he could perch high and be safe. But that wouldn't be like Banty, no. It would be like him to stand his ground and wait for the mink's challenge, to accept it and to fight to his death.

As I got close to the chicken lot, the stillness and the blinding snow bothered me. I stopped near the lot and listened. I couldn't see but a few yards in the pouring snow, but I listened. All I could hear was the uneasy muttering of the chickens.

I ran up to the chicken-lot fence. The big roosters and the hens were on the roosting poles and shivering, their heads turned sideways so they could see the ground with one eye.

I glanced about for Banty and called to him, but he did not answer me. Then I saw him. He stood over in one corner of the chicken lot, watching a hole under the chicken house. He stood poised for the fight. His neck was stretched out, and his feathers ruffled, and his eyes red like little sparks of fire.

I wanted to speak to Banty. I wanted to ask him,

what is it, little fellow? Get back. Let him poke out his head. Let me do it with the gun. He'll bite you through the neck.

But I couldn't explain all that to the little rooster. He stood there, shivering and waiting. I cocked my rifle. Maye I could get a shot at the mink when it came out of the hole to fight, and that way save the little rooster, but I didn't get the shot.

The mink struck so quick I got just a glimpse. The mink leaped for Banty's throat, and he almost got it, for when Banty knocked him loose with a spur, the mink was trying to spit red feathers out of his mouth, and he dashed in the hole again.

It hurt me in the heart when I saw blood trickling down Banty's red neck feathers while he stood poised again for the next strike.

And while I watched the fight, I remembered. I remembered that animals like minks that live in holes, their long suit is fighting in holes, and I could hear the mink's low, taunting, snarling growls. I knew the mink was daring the little rooster to get so mad he'd poke his head in the hole and get it bitten off.

But Banty knew better, for birds have to fight in the open, where they can use spur, beak, or claw.

By this time Banty was reeling and he seemed groggy. I did not think he'd live through the next strike of the mink, and I started to open the chicken-lot gate to get the little rooster and take him out of the fight. But before I could reach him, the mink struck again.

This time the mink leaped high as if to avoid Banty's spurs, but Banty bounced high, too, and the mink came with all his fury right into both of the little rooster's spurs, and fell back, and tried for his hole again, but couldn't make it.

Banty turned his head flat and looked at the mink with one eye. He seemed to know the fight was over, and he turned to me now. Maybe he'd known I was nearby all the time, but if so, he hadn't let on.

But now he came and rubbed against my legs, and tried to talk to me, and I reached down and picked him up and stroked his neck feathers.

I could feel his little heart pound fast against my body, and for a few minutes, the little rooster was hoarse from the bite in his neck. But he stretched his neck and twisted it, and worked it hard, for there was no give-up in his blood and bones, and I tried to help him. I gently rubbed his neck, and he'd hold still and let me, for he knew I was trying to help him.

When his voice came back, he raised his head high and proud, and he let go with a great crow that brought answers from the countryside farmyards, and it also brought the folks running from the house with sticks and brooms. The little rooster cringed and hugged close to me, but I stroked his feathers, and talked to him.

"Don't be afraid any more, Banty. I can talk for you. I can tell the folks it wasn't you that killed the chickens, and they won't hurt you now. . . ."

SEVEN SPEARS

RUTHERFORD MONTGOMERY

Tiki stood at the edge of the jungle, listening. He shaded his eyes. His three feet eight inches of height made it hard to see over the bush, and the sunshine hurt his eyes, for Tiki lived in the gloom of the great Ituri jungle.

Silently Tiki faded into the jungle. The green dusk swallowed his bare, brown body completely. High above his head flowers rioted in the sunshine, cling-

67

ing to the topmost branches of the giant trees. But in spite of the fragrance of the flowers, Tiki could smell the pungent taint of wild elephants.

He, Tiki, who had yet to win his place among the men of his clan, had located the elephants. He had done better than any of the men Igwa had sent out. Through him, the pygmy clan would be able to hunt the rogue elephant, the old female who had destroyed their village.

Tiki raised his small bow and tested the creeper which served as a bowstring. He laughed, but in laughing he made no sound. When he was a baby, he had been able to cry without making a sound. The little people of the Ituri jungle were a silent people, except when safe in a village. Tiki laughed because he was happy. He had located the elephants. Igwa would let him go with the hunters.

Wrinkling his nose, he listened. The sounds he heard were faint, the rustling of leaves as the elephants moved their huge ears. Then there was a rumbling sound, a loud sound which rolled through the jungle. The rumbling came from the stomach of one of the elephants. Tiki laughed again, his silent laugh. The old one could walk through the thickest bush without making a sound, but she could not keep her stomach from telling the world where she was hiding.

Moving silently as a leopard, Tiki ran through the green twilight. Once he halted to listen to sounds coming from beyond the green wall on his right. The sound was a loud drumming, which beat on his ears like heavy blows. Tiki usually ran away as fast as he could when he heard a gorilla drumming and bellowing, but today he had work to do.

Making sure there was no danger of meeting the old silver-back on the dim trail, Tiki ran on. Before he saw any of the elephants he smelled them, and then he heard the loud stomach rumblings. He counted the separate sounds. Five elephants, two old and three smaller. Tiki paused beside a giant tree.

A huge form loomed above him. He was standing within ten paces of the old female elephant. Her savage disposition caused the other elephants to let her stand alone. Tiki peered past her and saw a big bull and three smaller animals standing close together. The bull had a fine pair of tusks. Tiki looked up at the cow. Her tusks were not so good and would buy less salt and fewer arrow points, but she was the one they must kill, because she might return and attack the village again.

Tiki stood silently, checking the ground, planning the kill. Igwa would want to know how the beasts were standing, what the ground was like, where the trees stood, and how much open bush they would have to work in. Tiki fixed the scene in his mind before he turned away. When he did turn, he ran swiftly. Igwa and his hunting scouts had returned to the wrecked village. In passing along their small street, the old elephant had torn down every hut. She had not gotten her trunk on a single pygmy, because they had darted into the jungle when they first heard her savage screams. Already, the women and girls were rebuilding the huts, tying the bamboo canes together and covering the framework with leaves. They had been working less than an hour but most of the little houses were finished.

Igwa and his men were seated around a fire-pit. Their faces were gloomy. Then Tiki came running out of the jungle. No one asked any questions until Tiki had spoken, but the gloom vanished from their faces.

Tiki tried hard not to show how excited he was. "There are five. They sleep," he said.

Igwa got to his feet. He was the tallest man in the clan. He stood four feet five inches, weighed eighty-seven pounds.

"How do they sleep?" he asked.

Tiki described the elephants, how they stood, and where the trees stood, and when the open bush spread. When he had finished, Igwa nodded.

"We will take the seven spears." He smiled at Tiki. "You have earned a choice. What will you do?"

Tiki gripped his small bow. He pulled himself up very straight. "I will speak to the elephant," he said.

"That you have earned," Igwa agreed. Tiki was asking for the task Igwa usually performed himself because it was the most dangerous act of the elephant hunt. But Igwa was wise. Tiki might think better of his choice before long.

The hunters got to their feet. They picked up their little bows and examined the small metal points to make sure the poison was still on the blades. Seven of them picked up long spears tipped with iron blades. They looked at the blades to make sure they were well smeared with poison made from the roots of the *kilabo*.

Igwa led his men into the jungle. There were fourteen hunters, fourteen little brown fellows going out to kill a rogue elephant. They smiled as they moved into the warm gloom of the forest. They moved like silent shadows with Tiki leading the way.

Tiki led them in a circle to get the wind right. He remembered the gorilla and avoided that clearing. When he was near the elephants, he lifted one hand. The hunters crowded around Igwa and an excited talk took place, all through signs. Igwa settled the argument and gave a signal.

The small hunters moved toward the thick foliage which hid the elephants. When the seven spear men were ten paces from the sleeping female, they halted. She loomed above them, swaying gently back and forth, unaware of her danger.

No pygmy had strength enough to drive a spear through the tough old elephant's hide, but they had a plan. They planted their spears in the ground, with the blades slanting toward the elephant. They set them so close together there was barely room even for a pygmy to squeeze between the shafts. When the spears were set, they slipped back to where Igwa stood with the other hunters.

Igwa raised a hand. He looked at Tiki. Tiki smiled at him, but he was cold and was not sure he would be able to move. Igwa waited.

Tiki knew that if he did not move, Igwa would take his place, and everyone in the clan would know he was afraid. He looked at the sleeping elephant. Her stomach rumbled loudly. Her great tusks curved outward toward him. Tiki started to move toward the elephant.

When he reached the planted spears, he slipped between them. Slowly, he walked toward the huge beast. He was in the open now; the sun shone on his brown body. He halted just beyond reach of the deadly trunk.

With a loud yell, Tiki leaped in the air. He jumped up and down as he yelled. The elephant's eyes opened. Her trunk lifted and her great ears flapped. Her savage scream filled the jungle. Then she charged, her trunk reaching for the dancing little fellow who dared to challenge her.

Tiki whirled and fled. He ducked between the spears like a rabbit, then dodged to the right and dived into a bush. The instant he landed in the bush, he was up and away, darting and ducking. Behind him, the screams of the elephant had changed from angry squeals to the savage roar of a wounded beast. She had plunged upon the planted spears, and her own weight had done what the pygmies could never have managed to do.

Tiki circled and came back toward the scene of the attack. He found the hunters following the trail of the wounded elephant. Her companions had crashed away and were smashing down trees and brush far below. Igwa was listening. After a minute he gave a signal. The hunters started along the path the rogue elephant had made through the jungle.

The hunters ran along the trail for less than a half-mile before coming upon the elephant. Her great bulk lay at the foot of a tree. Igwa walked up to her and placed a bare foot against her side. When she did not move, a shout went up from the hunters. Little whistles were taken from thongs at the belts of the hunters. The jungle rang with their shrill piping. Soon the whistle signals were answered from the bush. The rest of the pygmies would soon arrive.

Tomorrow, there would be a great feast to celebrate the death of their enemy, the savage rogue elephant. And because the poison would not harm the meat, they would gorge themselves on elephant meat, which the pygmies consider a great delicacy.

Tiki climbed upon the mountain of meat and danced a little dance. From now on, he would be a hunter.

THE DAY THE COW SNEEZED

JAMES FLORA

I'll bet your cow never sneezed a hole in the school-house wall. Our cow did. Our old cow Floss sneezed so hard that she tore down the city hall, opened up the zoo, and scared the whole city of Sassafras Springs. All with one sneeze.

Of course it wasn't really old Floss's fault that she

sneezed so hard. My brother Fletcher is the one to blame.

Every morning before he goes to school, Fletcher takes our cow Floss down to the creek for a drink of water. One morning while old Floss was drinking, my brother Fletcher spied a little rabbit hopping across the pasture. He always wanted a pet rabbit, so he lit out after him. He chased it at least a mile, but he couldn't catch it because even a baby rabbit can run faster than a boy.

While he was gone, Floss drank too much water, and she got chilled standing in the cold creek. When Fletcher put her back in the barn, she was shaking and shivering.

She was shaking so much she could barely eat her morning hay. Her nose got redder and redder and began to itch. Her eyes watered. Her throat tickled. "K-k-k-k —"

"KA-CHOW" she sneezed.

A mouse was sleeping in Floss's hay. That powerful sneeze blew him right out of bed. The cat saw the mouse, leaped at it, missed, and landed on the billy goat.

When the billy goat felt the cat clawing at his back, he raced out of the barn and down the road in a fearful fright.

BAM! He bowled over the pig.

POW! He knocked down the mailman and the mailbox too.

CRASH! He bashed into a motorcyle policeman. The policeman fell off, and the billy goat landed on the motorcycle.

Down the road they flew, over the bridge, up the hill, through the woods, and over the cliff by Jack Makemson's barn.

They fell with a flip-flop and a loop-the-loop and landed on a steam roller.

Now everyone knows that a billy goat doesn't know how to drive a steam roller. Neither does a cat, nor a mouse for that matter. So the steam roller was able to go wherever it wanted, and away it went at full speed.

First it flattened a few trees. Then it mashed a street lamp, a fireplug, and a laundry truck. The mayor and the policeman tried to stop it, but they couldn't catch it.

The steam roller charged right on through the park and picked up a statue and a cannon. It knocked over City Hall and two stores. Then it tore right through the schoolhouse wall.

Fletcher was reciting in social studies, and when he saw our cat and our billy goat on the steam roller, he jumped on too and tried to stop it. But he couldn't find the right lever.

CRASH! They went through the other wall of the school and ripped down the street.

BING! BANG! SMASH! TINKLE!

Iron deer, picket fences, trains, gas stations, Good Humor trucks — everything was scrunched as flat as corn flakes.

KA-BLOWIE-BLAM!

They ripped through the fence around the zoo.

My, what a mess! They broke the cages, right and left, freeing all the animals. The elephant tried to stop the roller, but the roller was too strong, and it really changed the look of that elephant. In fact, the roller changed the looks of just about every animal in the zoo. It put a zigzag in the giraffe's neck. Flattened the moose's horns. Pressed a large alligator. Bent the rhino's snout. Curlicued the octopus. Made a crinkly lion and flattened a fat elephant.

All the other animals jumped on top of the steam roller as fast as they could. It was the only safe place to be.

"STOP!" everyone was shouting.

But the steam roller kept right on at full speed. It ran through the pond in the park and changed all of the fish. It mashed a tree and changed a few birds. Then it started for the merry-go-round.

WHAMBO! It missed the merry-go-round but crashed into the big Ferris wheel. All the animals and my brother Fletcher jumped and clutched at the seats of the big wheel.

They were happy to leave that crazy steam roller. They thought they were safe and sound, but the steam roller had knocked the big Ferris wheel off its base, and it started to roll away.

"WHOA-A-A!" shouted Fletcher, but the wheel was rolling so fast nobody could hold it. It ran over the popcorn, peanut, cotton candy, and lemonade stands, and food flew everywhere. At least they wouldn't be hungry.

Out of town they rolled and down a big hill, picking up speed.

People ran out of their houses. They thought a tornado was coming or that the moon had fallen. Cars and trucks stopped on the road, and the drivers dived into the ditches. Cows fainted. Horses ran away. It was a sight to see.

A big truck got tangled in the Ferris wheel and was carried along too. Fletcher didn't know what was in the truck until a little later when they scattered some Boy Scouts and rolled over their campfire.

ZIP! BLAM! ZOWIE!

Then he knew what was in the truck — fireworks for the Fourth of July. Great gobs of fireworks began to blow off. The noise was frightful. Fletcher had to stuff his fingers into his ears. It was so loud you couldn't have heard a lion roar if he had been sitting next to you.

The wheel raced through a farmyard zipping rockets through the barn.

Down the side of a mountain they rolled, faster and faster. At the bottom lay the Atlantic Ocean. Fletcher hugged a hippopotamus sitting next to him because hippos are very good swimmers.

CRUNCH! ZIP! SWISH!

The wheel rolled off the mountain onto a long dock. At the end of the dock was a fishing boat. The wheel rolled onto the boat, and out to sea they went scattering rockets right and left.

Fish popped their heads out of the water to see what was happening.

The fisherman who owned the boat telephoned for the fireboat to come to the rescue.

"HELLO! HELP!" he shouted into the phone. "A mountain full of monsters with fur hides and long snouts just stole my boat, and they are shooting cannon and squirting fire all over the ocean."

Fletcher's floating wheel was shooting so many rockets and fireworks that the fireboat couldn't get near them at first. Finally it dashed in with all nozzles squirting and splashed water all over Fletcher and his passengers and put out the fireworks.

When the fireboat came closer, the crew saw Fletcher

all wet and cold sitting there in that big wheel hugging a hippopotamus. They had to laugh. They roared and howled.

Then they took Fletcher and all of the animals to shore and sent them home in trucks.

When the truck came to our house, the driver climbed out and talked to Papa. While he talked, I could see Papa's face getting darker and darker, and I sure began to feel sorry for old Fletcher. When he finally climbed out of the truck, Papa took him by the ear. They marched into the barn and closed the door. I guess you know what happened to Fletcher in there.

I'll bet you my best jackknife that Fletcher won't be neglecting his duties and chasing rabbits again. He learned a lesson that day. He found out that a little teeny-weeny error can grow into a whopping big mistake almost before you can say

KA-CHOW!

THE BOTTOM OF THE BATTING LIST

MARION RENICK

The school that Mike went to was a small one. It was so small that one year there were only eight other boys in his class, and when spring came every one of those boys said Mike should play baseball.

"But I don't like baseball. I don't see any fun in it," Mike would tell them over and over.

The other boys always said, "How do you know? You've never played it."

Mike would dig his scuffed shoe into the gravel of

the school yard where the boys were holding practice. He would mutter, "Suppose I never have played. So what?" He would kick pebbles fiercely in all directions as if to show the fellows he was just as strong as they, even though he was so small for his age that they nicknamed him Mike, which was short for microbe.

"So what!" Mike would say.

"So it takes nine men to make a ball team, that's what!" Chick or Red or The Moose would answer. "And we've got nine fellows in our room *and we're going to have a team.*"

Mike knew it was no use to tell them to get somebody else. Each class always made up its own team and they played one another for the school championship. Naturally, as Chick said, it was better to have a poor player from your own room than a good player from some other class whose loyalty you couldn't count on.

Chick was the captain. He was one of the best players in school and, besides, he had a brother who played on the high school team. It was Chick who kept saying, "Come on, Mike. You don't want to spoil the fun for the rest of us, do you?"

Mike said, no, he didn't. Then The Moose spoke up, tugging thoughtfully at his large ears, which had won him his nickname. "You don't want those smarty-

pants 6A's to get ahead of us, do you? They're claim-
ing the championship, already."

Mike said, no, he didn't want the 6A's to get the
championship, but he just didn't like baseball.

"You'd like it, once you got a bat in your hand,"
Chick promised, "and learned how it feels to knock
out a good clean hit. One that, maybe, brings in a
couple of runs. You'd like baseball after that."

"Would I?" Mike asked. He brightened a little, hop-
ing Chick was right. He told himself that perhaps the
reason he didn't like baseball was because he never
had had a chance to play. Until this year there always
had been enough other boys — larger and stronger
than he — to make up the class team.

"Sure, you'd like it," Chick was saying. "Have you
ever swung a bat? Here, try this one."

Mike said, yes, he had swung a bat before. He took
the one Chick handed him, but he didn't say he had
one exactly like it at home. And a glove, too. He had
got them a long time ago but hadn't used them because nobody wanted him on a team. It was enough
to make a fellow not like baseball.

He stood there swinging the bat from his shoulder
and watching the boys. They were playing with two
bases, and when a man struck out he played in the
outfield until it was his turn to bat again. Everybody
had to take a turn at bat, even The Moose who was

pitcher. Chick said the only way a player could score a run was by making a hit and getting to first base before the baseman got there with the ball. And although the pitcher and catcher usually came at the bottom of the batting list, because they were expected to be the worst batters on any team, still Chick wanted them to be able to hit a pretty fair ball if the team got in a pinch.

Chick now took Red's place as catcher, squatting behind home plate, while Red hit a low ball to left field and streaked for first base.

"You're up next, Mike," Chick said. "Now, take it easy and keep your eye on the ball — then swing the old bat right out and sock it!"

The Moose sent over a slow one. Mike saw he'd have to step clear across the plate to reach it. But he missed it, even then.

"Jeepers!" Chick yelled. "What did you strike at that for? A ball has got to come directly over the plate — no lower than your knees and no higher than your shoulders — or it isn't any good. Didn't you know that?"

No, Mike didn't know that. He thought there must be an awful lot about baseball he didn't know. He'd have to watch very closely and learn the best he could, because he didn't want to ask questions or the fellows would think he didn't know *anything*.

"I get it now," he said, stepping back in position for the next pitch.

This time he was sure the ball was good. It was coming straight over the plate. He put everything he had into his swing, expecting to hear the bat crack sharply against the ball. But there came only the soft thud of the ball burrowing into the catcher's mitt. He could not believe he had missed. He turned around and looked. Yes, Chick had caught it, all right, and was laughing in a friendly way.

"Mike, you've got to keep your eye on the ball. Do you know what you did? You shut your eyes when the ball came close. How can you ever see to hit? Now try again — and watch the ball until your bat touches it."

The Moose threw another. An easy one, right at the bat. But before Mike had time to think, his eyes had closed and the ball plunked into the catcher's mitt.

"Three strikes and you're out!" Chick called. "Now go over there in right field, back of first base, and try to catch any balls the baseman misses."

"I'd better go home," Mike said. "There's a lot of stuff I want to do there. Besides, I don't think —"

"Jeepers! Anybody's liable to strike out his first time at bat," Chick said. "Just wait till you crack out a good clean hit. *Then* you'll think baseball's fun. All you need is practice."

Everybody agreed that all Mike needed was practice. That made good sense to Mike, too, so he stayed.

Although he struck out every time at bat, he came back for more the next day. And the day after that. By the time they played their first game, he still couldn't hit and he still thought baseball wasn't much fun, but his team needed nine boys so he had to stay. Chick put him at the bottom of the batting list.

Chick himself headed the batting list because he could almost always be counted on to get a hit and reach first base; next on the list came the three best hitters; then a couple more who were only so-so; then Red and The Moose; and at the bottom of the list, where he could do the least harm, was the poorest hitter on the team.

Mike nearly always struck out. "But you're getting better," Chick told him during their second game. "You're keeping your eyes on the ball now. Your only trouble is you can't put enough steam into your swing."

If Mike thought that was because he was smaller than the other boys, he did not mention the fact. He only said, rather eagerly, "I'm a pretty fast runner, Chick. I'll bet I could *steal* bases."

"You can't steal first base," Chick pointed out. "The only way you can get there is to bat a good ball. Or to bunt."

"What's a bunt?"

"It's a — well — watch me the next time I'm at bat. I'll bunt one for you," Chick said.

Presently Mike was up, with Red on second base

and The Moose on first. He knew that they hoped he would get a hit just this once. He spit on his hands, took a firmer grip on the bat and talked to himself. "Keep your eye on the ball," he said. "Sock it clear over that fence. You know you can do it if you swing hard enough."

Mike swung so hard he nearly lost his balance. But he didn't even touch the ball. Two more balls got past him the same way, and he went back to the bench. He was about to say that he didn't think baseball was much fun, when Chick spoke. "Watch this bunt, Mike."

The captain stepped up to the plate. Mike, watching every move, saw him turn to stand facing the pitcher just as the ball was thrown. Halfway stooping, Chick had the bat out in front of him, parallel with the ground, holding the handle with one hand and the center of the bat with the other. As the ball hit, it popped dully to the ground. The catcher scooped it up and sent it to first base, putting Chick out. But, Mike noticed, Chick's bunt had given Red time to move up from second to third base. Red was now in position to come in home for a run, if the next batter got a hit. The Moose was on second.

"I get it," Mike said as Chick came back to the bench. "From now on, I'll bunt. If I can't hit hard and get to first base myself, maybe I can help some other player to come in home."

"Bunting isn't as easy as it looks," Chick warned.

"You'd better learn to bat first."

But from then on Mike was on the lookout for every bunt, trying to find out how it was done. He had been put in the right fielder's position for the same reason he was at the bottom of the batting list. Very few balls ever came into his territory, so he had lots of time on his hands out there. At first, he had spent it thinking how dull baseball was, but now he was too busy watching for bunts to remember he didn't like the game.

He studied bunting for four or five games; he even practiced secretly, throwing a rubber ball against the side of the garage at home and trying to bunt it as it bounced back. He thought he had mastered all the tricks of bunting by the time his team was ready for their last game — the game with the 6A's, the game that would decide the school championship.

Of course the 6A's were bragging and blowing as though they had won already, but Mike's team felt they had a fair chance, themselves, although they did not say much. The whole school took sides, with a great deal of arguing about whether The Moose could out-pitch the 6A man and whether a player like Mike was too big a handicap for any team to overcome. Both teams agreed to ask Chick's older brother to umpire. The game was that important.

Chick's brother brought another high school ball player to assist him. Having these two older men there, marking off the diamond in the gravelly play yard, placing the bases in position, now and then consulting the baseball rule books that bulged their hip pockets, seemed to put the game into the big leagues. Even Mike, taking his starting position in right field, began to feel some excitement about baseball as he planned how he would bunt when his turn came.

But Mike didn't get to bat in the first inning. The 6A pitcher was too good. He sent a ball over the plate so fast that even Chick and the fellows at the top of the batting list couldn't touch it. Mike was worried. He knew he never could bunt a ball like that.

Neither team scored in the first inning, but the 6A's got two runs in the second, while Mike's team got one. In the third, the 6A's ran wild and brought in five runs, which so discouraged Mike, who was first up at bat, that he thought it no use even to try a bunt. He swung half-heartedly at the first ball, missing it by a mile. The second ball came more slowly and, after it passed, he realized he might have bunted it successfully if he hadn't been expecting one too fast to be hit. The third pitch was wide. But Mike had long since learned to strike only at balls that came over the plate, so he let it go by. One of the umpires yelled, "Ball one!"

Another ball came over, too low. "Ball two!" called the umpire. The pitcher was slowing down now. Or, Mike wondered, was he merely resting his pitching arm? After all, a smart pitcher doesn't waste his fast balls on a fellow who is at the bottom of the batting list.

"I'll show him," Mike muttered. "I'll give him the old bunt."

Then Mike had a crafty thought. Why throw away a bunt when there were no men on base? Why not go on striking out until the pitcher felt sure he had nothing to worry about when Mike was at bat? Then —

"*Then* — I'll show him," Mike said to himself. And struck out.

His team got in three runs that inning. The score was 7 to 4 in favor of the 6A's as they went into the fourth. Then Chick passed the word around to tighten up. So, with The Moose already on first base, Mike went to bat determined to do his best for his team.

Not until he stood at the plate waiting for the pitch did he realize how little he knew about bunting. Two slow, easy balls got past him before he was sure what he was trying to do. When the third ball came, he was ready with the bat in the correct position — but he forgot to slide his right hand out to support the center of it. At just the wrong moment the bat wobbled and let the ball go by.

As Mike returned to the bench he was telling himself baseball wasn't any fun. But he was remembering in the back of his mind how the whole 6A team had seemed to relax and go off guard when he came to bat. He was thinking, too, how to use his right hand to steady the bat. He smiled to himself.

The 6A's got one run in the fourth and one in the fifth. Mike's team got two in the fourth, which left them trailing, 9 to 6, when they went to bat in the second half of the fifth inning. Their first man up hit a single and got on first base. They were near the bottom of the batting list now, but luckily Red and The Moose each got a hit. That left all three men on base when Mike came up.

"Bases loaded," Mike said to himself. "Boy, what a spot for a bunt!"

He was too excited to let the first ball go by, as more experienced players sometimes do. He saw the pitcher raise his arm, and the instant the ball was in the air Mike had turned to face it, holding the bat across in front of him. Plunk! The ball hit squarely. Mike felt a sharp, stinging pain in the fingers of his right hand but didn't have time to think about it as he flung aside the bat and raced down the base line. The 6A's had been caught completely off guard. By the time the catcher had recovered the ball and decided where to throw it, Mike was safe. Red and The Moose had advanced to next base, and the man on third had got home. Mike had brought in a run! He stood on first base and hugged himself with excitement.

Chick batted next. He was put out by the first baseman, but meantime Red got home. Two runs in!

The next batter struck out, and the one after him hit to center field, giving The Moose time to get to home plate. Mike, who had stolen up from second base to third, was right on his heels and got in safe, too. For the first time in his life, Mike had made a run! He was so thrilled and worked up and breathless, he didn't notice anything the matter until Chick exclaimed, "Jeepers, Mike, what happened to your hand?"

Mike looked. Blood was splattered all down the front of him, even dripping on the ground. He couldn't tell for sure how many fingers were hurt because his whole hand was covered with blood.

"Jeepers!" Chick said again in an awed voice.

Another man had struck out by that time and the inning ended. Chick's brother, taking one look at Mike's hand, brought the first-aid kit. But although the umpires discovered no broken bones and found that the injury was much more painful than it was serious, they decided Mike should have a doctor dress it immediately. "Better be on the safe side," they said.

"What's the score?" Mike asked.

"It's 10 to 9, our favor," his teammates told him.

"I'll keep on playing," he decided. "If I leave now we'll have to give the game to the 6A's because we won't have enough men to make a team."

"But the game is over," Chick's brother said, much to the boy's surprise. "You have played five innings, haven't you?" He brought the rule book from his pocket. He thumbed the pages and let Chick and Mike and all the 6A's read the lines he pointed out. There it was in black print: "It is a regulation game if, after five innings have been played, the game is called off by the umpires on account of rain, darkness, or any other cause which stops play."

The other umpire agreed. "Certainly when one team has only eight men to put in the field, that is a cause which stops play."

"And five innings have been played, all right," Mike's teammates were declaring happily. "So we won — by one run. Your run, Mike!" They pounded him on the back and capered around, demanding of the 6A's, "Ho, ho, who're the champions now?"

The other team made a great fuss, but they had to admit the umpires were right. While they were still arguing, Chick, on his brother's advice, steered Mike out of the school yard and down the street to the nearest doctor's office.

Mike's hand was hurting more and more. He had to grit his teeth to keep from groaning as he tried to apologize, "I'm sorry I spoiled the game."

"You didn't spoil it!" Chick fairly shouted. "You won it! We never could have kept ahead of those 6A's for four more innings. You really won the game with your smashed hand. By the way, how did it happen? When you bunted?"

Mike nodded, a little grim and white about his tightly closed lips.

"I was afraid of that," Chick sympathized. "You have to learn to keep your fingers out of the way, where the ball won't hit them."

"I get it now," Mike said. He even managed to smile at himself, wondering how he had missed such an important point when he watched the other fellows bunting. Perhaps he should have asked questions, after all.

"But, Jeepers, it sure was a swell bunt." Chick's face glowed. "You picked a smart time to use it, too — with the bases loaded."

Mike tried to look modest, but he didn't feel modest in the least. He felt awfully proud of himself. He had won the game. Single-handed. Hadn't Chick just said so? Baseball *was* fun!

HENRY'S DOG HENRY

WALTER R. BROOKS

There was a boy named Henry Tanner, and his uncle sent him a cocker spaniel. He had a hard time thinking up a name for the dog. His mother said: "Well, you can name him anything you want to. What name do you like best?"

"I like my own name best," said Henry.

"But you can't call him 'Henry,'" said his mother.

Henry thought a minute and then he said, "Well, I don't know why not. I think it would be fun if we both had the same name." So he called the dog Henry.

It worked at first, because when Henry (the boy) called, "Henry!" Henry (the dog) came. And when Mrs. Tanner called "Henry!" they both came.

But there began to be mix-ups. Sometimes when Mrs. Tanner said, "Henry, do this," or "Henry, do that," the wrong one did it. Like the time Mrs. Tanner was going out for the evening, and she left the house she called out, "Henry, you go straight to bed at nine o'clock."

So Henry (the dog) went and curled up on his piece of carpet back of the stove at nine, but Henry (the boy) was still up when his mother got home, and he said, "Why, Mother, I thought you meant Henry. You said 'Henry.' "

Mrs. Tanner was a fair-minded woman, and she said, "Well, I guess I ought to have said *which* Henry. But you go straight to bed now."

The trouble was that Mrs. Tanner was sort of absent-minded, and couldn't seem to remember to say which Henry she meant. And Henry (the dog) was a well-trained dog and always minded and did what he was told. So pretty soon all the minding in the house was done by Henry (the dog).

"Henry," Mrs. Tanner would say, "go get me my sewing basket from upstairs." And Henry (the dog) would go get it, while Henry (the boy) would pretend that he hadn't heard anything.

Now Henry (the dog) didn't mind doing all these things, but he realized that Henry (the boy) was getting pretty lazy.

"Pretty soon," he thought, "that boy won't do anything for himself. He'll be just a shiftless no-account, who'll expect everybody else to do his work for him, and nobody will like him and he won't have any friends. And I don't want to belong to a boy that nobody likes." So he began to think what he could do to help Henry.

Of course, Mrs. Tanner didn't like the way things were going either, and when Henry (the dog) did something that she had asked Henry (the boy) to do, she scolded him. And he would put his tail between his legs and crouch down, apologizing in dog language. But he went right on minding just the same, because he knew if he didn't Henry would be mad at him.

His chance came that night after supper when Mrs. Tanner called, "Henry, there's fifty cents on my dresser if you want to go to the movies."

Henry (the boy) didn't hear her, and Henry (the dog) dashed upstairs and took the fifty-cent piece in his mouth and ran down to the movie.

Well, Miss Schmitt, who was cashier at the movie theater, was pretty surprised when a dog stood up on his hind legs and dropped fifty cents on the little shelf. She jumped and her eyes popped. She knew that her job was to sell all the tickets she could so she grabbed the fifty cents. Then she hesitated and said, "Well, I guess you're under fifteen, aren't you?" and she shoved back a quarter and gave him a ticket.

So Henry went in and gave up the ticket and bought a bag of popcorn. The ticket taker and the popcorn man were so surprised that I guess they didn't realize that Henry was a dog until he had gone in and taken a seat.

The show had started so it was dark and nobody noticed much when the dog sat down. He just sat there and watched the show, and one or two people said, "For Pete's sake, look at that dog!" But that was all. And when the show was over he trotted back home.

But Henry was mad at him. He never licked the dog, but he threatened him, and he said, "You've done me out of a good show. You took that money even though you knew it was meant for me. Now you leave things like that alone, do you understand?" "Well, I can't do that again," Henry (the dog) said to himself. "I thought if I did something like that he'd be afraid to have me answer, and when Mrs. Tanner called, 'Henry!' he'd run to answer himself."

One day Henry's uncle came to visit, and, of course, he wanted to see the dog he'd given him.

"What did you name him?" he asked, and Henry said, "Henry."

Well, the uncle thought that was pretty funny and he said, "Good grief, why didn't you give him a regular dog's name? Like — lemme see — well, say 'Rover'?"

"Golly, I wish he had!" Henry (the dog) thought, and he was so pleased at the idea that he wagged his tail hard and went over and licked the uncle's hand.

"There — see?" said the uncle. "He likes a regular dog name. Hey, Rover?"

Henry (the dog) didn't like "Rover," he thought it was terrible. But he thought, "Boy, this is my chance!" and when the uncle said "Rover" the second time he jumped up and down and barked his pleased bark.

"See?" said the uncle, "He likes it."

"Well, I don't," said Henry (the boy). "Here, Henry. Come here, pup."

But the dog paid no attention.

"Henry!" said the boy. "Come here!"

But the dog didn't even look around.

"You haven't trained him very well," said the uncle. "Doesn't even know his own name."

"He does too!" said Henry, and he kept on trying, and even slapped the dog, which was something he had never done before. But Henry (the dog) just lay down and went to sleep. But when the uncle said something about Rover, he jumped up and went to him and put his head on his knee.

By and by the uncle went back to Buffalo, where he lived. Then Henry's (the boy's) troubles began. Henry (the dog) wouldn't do anything that Henry (the boy) told him to. He acted as if he'd never heard the name Henry before. And when Henry (the boy) yelled at him, he just looked bewildered.

Of course this meant that when Mrs. Tanner said, "Henry, do this," or "Henry, do that," Henry (the boy) waited a minute. Then when Henry (the dog) just sat there and didn't even twitch a whisker, Henry (the boy) got up and did what his mother asked him to.

Pretty soon Henry (the boy) was doing quite a lot of minding — even some that belonged to Henry (the dog). Mrs. Tanner would say, "Henry, take that bone outdoors," and when the dog didn't do anything about it, the boy would pick it up and carry it out. He even began doing things before he was told to.

Well, Henry (the dog) was pretty pleased. He had a friend, Jock, a Scotty with whom he often went rabbit hunting. There weren't any rabbits around that neighborhood, but they had fun hunting them just the same. He said to Jock, "That Henry, he's going to turn out all right. He's the kind of boy now that a dog could be proud to belong to."

"Yeah?" said Jock. "The way I heard it yesterday, he says you don't mind any more and he's going to give you away."

"I know," said Henry sadly. "But what can I do? If I start answering to the name of Henry again, we'll be right back where we were."

"If he wasn't so dumb," Jock said, "he'd try calling you other names."

"I know," Henry said again. "But we can't expect a boy to be as smart as we are. Boys just aren't very bright. They talk a lot, but they don't think much. They aren't like dogs."

I guess things might have ended pretty badly for Henry (the dog) if he had been right about boys. But Henry (the boy) really had been thinking. He was pretty fond of his dog, and it made him unhappy that they couldn't seem to get along. And one afternoon he was sitting on the back steps. Henry (the dog) was lying on the grass.

The boy looked at the dog and thought, "I wish I knew why he acts so funny and won't mind any more. We used to have a lot of fun. My goodness, he hasn't wagged his tail since Uncle George was here. That was when Uncle George called him Rover. Rover!" the boy said disgustedly.

He was so disgusted that he said it out loud. To his amazement, the dog jumped up and began to bark and wag his tail.

Henry stared at him and said, "Well, hey! What goes on here?" Then he frowned thoughtfully and picked up a stick and threw it. "Go get it, Henry!" he said. And the dog lay down and pretended to go to sleep.

"Go get it, Rover!" said Henry. And the dog ran and got the stick, and then he pranced around and barked shrill little excited barks until Henry said, "All right, all right. Don't have hysterics. It's a silly name, if you ask me, but you're the one who has to answer to it. Come on, Rover. Let's take a walk."

So that was the end of the trouble, and Henry and Rover had good times together again. Of course, being so absent-minded, Mrs. Tanner couldn't remember half the time that Henry (the dog) was now Rover, and she was a little surprised sometimes to see her son doing something that she thought she had told the dog to do.

Once, when a Mrs. Haskell came in to call, and Henry and Rover were sitting on the davenport, she said, "Henry, get right down off those cushions," and the boy got down on the floor, but the dog stayed where he was.

Mrs. Haskell said, "Gracious! Gracious!" But Mrs. Tanner just said, "Oh dear, I don't know how it is I always get those two mixed up." Mrs. Haskell gave her a funny look, and didn't stay very long, and she never came back again. But Mrs. Tanner didn't care, for she wasn't too absent-minded to realize that Henry was minding a lot better than he used to.

Rover (formerly Henry) was happy, too. Even when Jock, and other dogs of his acquaintance, laughed at his new name and jeered at him on the street, and said, "Oh, see Rover! Oh, see the pretty doggie-woggie!" Even then he didn't care. He didn't even bother to bark at them. And as it isn't fun to tease anybody who doesn't notice it, pretty soon they stopped.

BIG RIG

BILL and ROSALIE BROWN

Clarence Carter was mad when he pulled into the Chicago truck terminal with a load of freight from Detroit. He was mad, but he was on time.

Clarence was always on time. He had never been late with a load of freight and he had never had an accident on the highway. He was the best big-rig driver the company had.

Clarence drove slowly through the yard, past other trucks and trailers, past the sheds where men were

104

washing the big rigs with a steam hose, past the shops where mechanics were repairing engines and changing tires. The men all waved to him or shouted, "Hi, Clarence!"

Clarence didn't wave back. He didn't call "Hi!" to anyone. He wore his driver's cap, with its safe-driving pin, pulled down square on his head, and he looked straight in front of him.

The dispatcher came out of his office. He motioned to a man driving a small machine called a yard mule.

"Hey! Unhook Clarence's tractor!" he said. "Put the trailer in Dock A and get her unloaded."

Clarence climbed down from the cab. He was frowning.

"Well, what's wrong with you?" the dispatcher said.

"If that mouse is in my rig again, I'll quit," Clarence said.

"Mouse? What mouse?"

"What mouse! The mouse that's trying to make me lose my job, that's what mouse!"

"Hm," the dispatcher said. "Never heard of a mouse in a big rig before. What did he do?"

"It's all on my report," Clarence said. "Last trip, one package of salted peanuts nibbled. Mouse damage, ten cents. Trip before that, one box of soda crackers entered and gnawed. Damage, thirty cents. Before that, one salami chewed up!"

The dispatcher laughed. "Oh, is that all?"

"What do you mean is that all? When customers ship freight by truck, they count on the driver to get it through in good shape, not mouse-gnawed."

The dispatcher scratched his head, and looked over at the dockwallopers who were unloading Clarence's trailer.

"Why don't you set a trap for him?" he asked.

"I've set wire traps and I've set spring traps," Clarence said. "I've set box traps and I've set booby traps. A spring trap snipped off one of his ears. Now he won't go near a trap!"

The dispatcher shook his head. "I guess he just likes you, Clarence. But maybe you could get away from him. You've been a long time on the Chicago-Detroit run. We could give you a different route."

"You mean. . . . . run away?"

The dispatcher shrugged. "Why not? I could give you a rig headed for Salt Lake, or maybe clear to the West Coast."

"Yeh!" Clarence pointed his finger at the dispatcher. "I'll go West, that's what I'll do. You give me a rig headed west. I don't care if she's a bull hauler or a bobtail or a rag top. I'll go so far west I'll never hear of that mouse again!"

The dockwalloper came out of the trailer of Clarence's rig holding two books, one in each hand.

"Hey, Carter!" the dockwalloper yelled. "A mouse ate the backs off six copies of *Mother Goose!*"

The mouse was Angelo. His whiskers were bent and he had lost one ear in Clarence's mousetrap. Angelo looked as if he'd been around, and he had. He had spent summers in Maine, and winters in Florida. He had climbed into a big rig in New Orleans, and traveled all the way to New England in a bale of cotton. Then he traveled from New England to Chicago in a load of new overalls.

At Chicago in the loading terminal, just five days ago, Angelo had first seen Clarence. Angelo had been peeking out of a crack in one of the loading docks. He had seen the kind look on Clarence's face, and the safe-driving button on Clarence's cap.

There's the driver for me, Angelo had thought. I'll follow him wherever he goes.

Angelo loved the big rigs Clarence drove. He liked the hum of the fourteen giant tires on the pavement. He loved the smell of exhaust fumes from the diesel engine. He thought it was sweeter than salami or Limburger cheese.

Sometimes the truck would be loaded with stoves and refrigerators. It might carry shoelaces, or roller skates, or wastebaskets. Angelo liked to poke around and see what there was. Once he came to a cardboard carton, and when he gnawed through the cardboard, he found soda crackers.

This is a nice life for a mouse, Angelo thought.

The day Clarence decided to go West, Angelo was

waiting for him, just as he always was. He watched
Clarence talking to the dispatcher, and the dispatcher
talking to Clarence. He watched from the middle of
a pile of paper sacks on the warehouse floor. He noticed everything carefully, trying to find out which
truck Clarence was going to drive this time.

The terminal was noisy. Little loading tractors
buzzed in every direction with stacks of cartons. Some
men pushed hand trucks. All along the loading docks
huge trailers were being filled by the dockwallopers
with cartons, crates, and bundles.

Clarence and the dispatcher walked along the dock,
looking over the different rigs. They came to a refrigerator truck. The trailer was large and had a small
box with slots high up on the front. This was the
cooler for the warm refrigerator coils.

"Hey," Clarence said "where's this reefer going?"

"It's taking frozen foods to Salt Lake City," the dispatcher said.

Clarence walked around to the back of the trailer
and looked inside. He saw frost on the walls and ice
on the ceiling.

"A mouse would get mighty cold in there," he said.
"Who's driving this reefer?"

"Old Spook Martin," the dispatcher said.

"Hm." Clarence rubbed his chin. "I think maybe
if it's all right with you and old Spook Martin, I'll
drive this rig."

Angelo had ridden in big dry vans, on flat racks, and open tops, but he had never ridden in a refrigerator truck. He slipped inside just before the dispatcher told the men to close the doors and seal them.

"She's all buttoned up!" the dock checker called. Clarence drove off.

Angelo knew getting into a refrigerator truck was a mistake before he was half a mile on the road to Salt Lake City. Frost was thick on the walls, and there was frost on the boxes of frozen food. It was dark inside the refrigerator truck and so cold that Angelo's one ear was getting numb.

Angelo decided he'd better run around and warm up, but he couldn't move. He pulled and tugged, but his tail was frozen to the floor. He pulled and pulled till the skin of his tail almost came off. Finally he pulled loose.

Angelo explored the refrigerator truck, hunting for a way out. He looked everywhere along the walls. The reefer was well sealed so that it would stay freezing cold. There wasn't a crack around the doors to let in warm air.

Angelo started to climb up over the packages of frozen string beans and fish sticks toward the top of the trailer. Up in front he could hear the humming of the refrigerator motor over the hum of the tires on the highway. Then he saw a tiny crack of light near the roof.

The mouse pressed his nose and whiskers to the crack. It was a hole where the refrigeration tubing went through, and there was soft rubber around the tubes to keep the air out. Angelo squeezed past the rubber. He found himself in the box that contained the warm coils. He lay down on the coils. Through the ventilators he could see the country go by.

This is just like Florida, Angelo thought. And he could go back into the refrigerator any time he was hungry.

Clarence would drive eight or ten hours, then sleep in a motel. Then he would drive another shift. At last he pulled his big rig into the freight yard at Salt Lake City.

"Somewhere back in that trailer, there may be a frozen mouse," he called to the yardman. "Don't get him mixed up with the sausages."

Clarence went off to eat. When he came back his rig was unloaded. A dockwalloper stuck his head out of the back of the reefer.

"We didn't find a mouse, frozen or alive," he said, holding up a package, "but we found these fish sticks chewed open."

Clarence threw his driver's cap on the ground and stamped on it.

"Where's the dispatcher?" he yelled. "I'll ask him to give me a tanker. I'll take a tank truck across the desert. I'd like to see a mouse that can live in one of those!"

The dispatcher assigned Clarence to a tanker loaded with molasses. It was headed for San Francisco and Clarence could drive it clear through.

"It's a pajama wagon — there's a bed in the back, so you can sleep right on the road. It's mostly desert now until you get to the mountains. This isn't the time of year for flash floods or sandstorms, so you shouldn't have any trouble — at least until you reach the mountains."

"How about places to eat?" Clarence asked.

"Few and far between," the dispatcher said.

"Best one's Ma Bentley's just before you reach the mountains. Won't get there until tomorrow night, though."

Clarence got a good sleep in a motel room, bought a couple of ham sandwiches in a paper bag for emergency rations, and went back to the terminal for his tanker. It was all loaded with molasses and ready to go.

From a hiding place under the loading dock, Angelo was watching Clarence. He set his bag of sandwiches down on the pavement, climbed into the cab and started the engine to warm it up. He climbed out again and walked around the truck. He checked the air brakes, he checked the red stop lights and he checked the amber clearance lights. He checked the air pressure in the tires. He checked the horn and it blasted out so loud and sudden that it made Angelo's whiskers quiver.

While Clarence was busy checking the tanker, Angelo was busy trying to get inside it. There weren't any doors and there weren't any ventilators. There were only connections for hoses.

Angelo looked up at the cab. It was very high up and the doors were closed. This time Angelo thought he was going to be left behind.

Then Angelo's nose began to twitch. There was something good close by— the smell of fresh ham sandwiches. Angelo was hungry because he hadn't eaten anything since the fish sticks.

A corner of the paper bag was open. In one jump, Angelo was in with the sandwiches. Even before he could gnaw through one of the wax-paper wrappings, Clarence had picked up the bag, twisted the top closed tight and tossed it into the cab.

Clarence climbed up into the truck. He put the lunch bag in the metal toolbox behind him and slammed down the lid. He put the truck in low gear and it moved slowly out of the freight yard on the long run to San Francisco.

The load of molasses was heavy. The tanker growled along, picking up speed as Clarence shifted. Slowly he pulled out of town, past the last service stations. The highway straightened out across the desert covered with sagebrush. A jack rabbit hopped across the road. Clarence slowed down a little so that he wouldn't run over it.

Clarence drove and then slept, stopped for a quick meal, then drove and slept. Once when he was nearly asleep in the bunk behind the seat, he thought he heard a rustling in the toolbox, but then he thought, that mouse had really got on his nerves.

About noon the second day, Clarence saw the mountains standing up blue ahead of him, and he knew he had just about crossed the big desert. He could see the glistening white snow on the peaks. Clusters of storm clouds were gathering around the mountains.

Clarence knew it was dangerous for a sleepy driver to drive a big rig — particularly over dangerous mountains. He would take a few hours' sleep, then get a good dinner and push over the mountains in the night.

Clarence pulled his rig onto a wide turnout. He remembered the ham sandwiches he had bought in Salt Lake City. They would be stale, but they would hold him until dinnertime. He opened the toolbox and pulled out the paper bag. He shoved his hand into it for a sandwich. His hand touched something furry and wiggling. He grabbed at it. He pulled it out of the bag and held it high. He had a mouse by the tail. The mouse had only one ear.

"So that's what you look like!" Clarence said.

Angelo wriggled and tried to get away.

"Oh, no you don't!" Clarence growled. "You've had your last ride in a big rig." He held the mouse up by his tail in front of his face.

For once in his life, Angelo was scared. Hanging there by his tail, he looked at Clarence's upside-down face. Even upside down, the face didn't look mean.

Clarence waggled his finger right in front of Angelo's whiskers.

"I really should feed you to a bobcat after all the trouble you caused me."

Clarence could feel Angelo shudder right up through his tail.

"I know what I'll do," Clarence said. "I'll maroon you out here in the desert. The sun will bake you all day and the wind will freeze you all night and the coyotes will chase you from one clump of sagebrush to another. How do you like that?'

Angelo twisted around and looked out over the desert upside down. The sagebrush was where the sky should be and the mountains in the distance pointed straight down.

Clarence got out and started to put Angelo down on a rock. Then he saw a black hawk circling overhead. Clarence wouldn't even be back in his truck before that hawk would swoop down on the mouse.

Clarence shook his head. "You're a no-good, one-eared pest," he said to Angelo, "but I can't stand bloodshed." He started for the truck, carrying the mouse by the tail. "Come on, I'll find someplace else to leave you. I'll leave you in some restaurant where you'll get plenty to eat."

Clarence put Angelo back in the bag with the sandwiches so that he wouldn't be hungry, shut the bag up in the toolbox and went to sleep.

It was almost dark when Clarence woke. He pulled the rig out onto the highway and headed toward the mountains again.

Cars and trucks had their lights on now, and the first truck that Clarence met flicked its lights twice, then twice more. That was a new signal to Clarence. He knew most of the truckers' signals. When a truck came up behind another truck and flicked its lights once, that meant it wanted to pass. The other truck flicked its lights to show it was safe to pass.

There were other signals, too. Three blinks of the lights was a signal that there was danger ahead— a wreck, a washed-out bridge, or a landslide. But this signal — two blinks, and then two more — was a new one. And Clarence knew that truckers didn't use light signals except for something important.

In the next half hour, Clarence met two more trucks and both of them gave the same signal. Something was up there ahead of him. Clarence knew that, but he didn't know what it was.

It was dark now and Clarence couldn't see the towering mountains that lay ahead, but far down the highway he could see the bright lights of a truck-stop restaurant.

He could stop there for dinner and find out from

other truckers what the signals meant. And this would be the place to leave the mouse behind.

Two other trucks were pulled up in front of Ma Bentley's truck-stop restaurant. They were lighted up like Christmas trees with red and amber lights.

Clarence brought his big rig to a stop. The air brakes sighed. He locked the engine in low gear and climbed out to put blocks under the wheels so that there would be no chance of a runaway.

Then Clarence climbed back into the cab and lifted the lid of the toolbox. He took out the paper bag that held what was left of the ham sandwiches. He looked inside. The mouse was trying to hide among the sandwich wrappings at the bottom.

"This is the end of the line for you," Clarence said. "You'll find a good home in this restaurant, if you behave yourself and don't make trouble."

Clarence twisted the top of the bag tight again and took it with him into the restaurant.

It was steamy and warm in Ma Bentley's restaurant. Clarence could smell beef stew and coffee. He could smell hamburgers frying with onions. He could also smell fresh, hot doughnuts.

Two other truck drivers were perched up on yellow stools at the counter. Clarence found a stool and sat down. Ma Bentley put a glass of water, a knife, fork and spoon in front of him. Clarence ordered beef stew, coffee and two doughnuts. He set the bag with the mouse in it on the stool beside him.

Clarence turned to the other drivers.

"Can one of you gear jammers let me in on a secret? What kind of a signal is two and two blinks?"

The driver sitting next to Clarence looked up, surprised.

"You new here?"

Clarence nodded. "Just out from Chicago."

The driver leaned toward the driver at the end of the counter.

"Hey, Buckeye," he said, jerking his head toward Clarence. "New man. Wants to know what kind of a signal two and two is."

Buckeye looked Clarence over carefully.

"You mean, blink, blink — blink, blink — like that?"

"That's right," Clarence said. "Blink, blink — blink, blink."

"That means snow on the mountain," Buckeye said. "It means to put iron on your tires. It means the guy who gave you the signal got through, but he's warning you."

Clarence scowled a little. "Well, I'm not the kind of driver who likes to risk his rig," he said. "And it would be nice sitting out the storm right here. . . ." He glanced down at the bag with the mouse in it. He could hear Angelo rustle a little. "But I've got to get through tonight," he said firmly. "I've just got to."

Buckeye picked up a toothpick. "What kind of cargo have you got that's so all-fired important?"

"A mouse," Clarence said. "I mean . . . molasses!"

"Molasses!" Buckeye snorted. "Molasses won't spoil overnight."

The first driver swung around on his stool toward Clarence.

"Did you ever hear of Highgear Higgins? He tried to get through the pass in the blizzard of '56. Jack-knifed his rig in a snowbank right at the top. Old Highgear was there for three days before the snow-plows got him out. He had nothing to eat but a cargo of canned tomatoes and he had to open the cans with a jack handle."

Clarence took a swallow of coffee. "I've got chains and I'm used to snow around Chicago," he said.

"The school bus was the last to go through," Ma Bentley said, "and that was about four o'clock."

"Well, if a school bus can do it, my rig can do it," Clarence said. He paid for his meal, glanced down at the bag with the mouse in it, and went out into the cold night to put chains on his rig.

Back in the restaurant, Ma Bentley picked up her broom and came out from behind the counter to sweep the floor. She walked over to the window and rubbed a clear place on the steamy glass with her apron. She could see Clarence putting the chains on his rig. Already a few snowflakes were drifting down. She shook her head.

"It's beginning to snow even down here," she said. She saw Clarence's bag on the stool. "Oh, dear, that poor man left his lunch."

She picked up the bag and hurried back behind the counter. "I'll drop half a dozen fresh doughnuts in here," she said. "I don't want to think of that nice fellow maybe stuck up there in a snowdrift with nothing to eat but molasses."

She twisted the top of the bag closed. "Here, Buckeye," she said, tossing him the bag. "Just drop this in the cab of that fellow's truck when you go out. He'll never even know he forgot it."

As Clarence headed into the mountains he could feel the wheels of the big rig crunching the snow. He knew the brittle sound of the chains as the drive wheels gripped the ice on the pavement. He could feel it, too, when the wheels slipped. Then the wheels gripped again and the rig crept forward. The headlights hardly picked up the white road ahead because of the driving snow. There were no automobile tracks to follow.

What can I say, Clarence thought, if anything goes wrong with the rig? I *can't* say I drove over the mountains at night to get rid of a mouse.

Clarence knew one thing. He would be the last truck over that road until the blizzard ended and the

snowplows cleared it. He thought about Highgear
Higgins, and how he spent three days in a snowdrift
eating canned tomatoes.

The drive wheels began to spin again, and the
truck started to slip sideways in the snow.

"Whoa, old horse," Clarence said. 'Easy now," and
he spun the steering wheel and straightened up the
truck before it slid off the road.

Clarence dimly made out a highway marker. The
top of the mountain was only a quarter of a mile
farther.

The howling wind was drifting snow across the
road, but it was still light enough to push through,
and the wheels packed it down. Some of the drifts
beside the road looked deep enough to bury a big
rig. In spite of the warm cab, just looking at the cold
drifts and swirling snow made Clarence shiver.

Angelo had eaten all the doughnuts he could by
this time, and he was tired of being shut up in the
paper bag. He gnawed a hole in the paper and crawled
out. For a while he sat quietly on the toolbox. The
noise of the engine was loud.

Angelo saw Clarence's face in the dim glow of the
dashboard light and it looked worried, but Angelo
didn't worry. Now that he had ridden in the cab of
a truck, he decided it was the best place of all to ride
— right up near his good friend, Clarence. He thought

he would find a good hiding place there to make a den.

Angelo found a nice place up behind the dashboard where there was a tangle of wires. He turned around a few times. This is just right, he thought, but there are too many wires.

Two wires, especially, were in the way. Angelo began to gnaw on them. The insulation came off easily, but Angelo nearly broke his teeth on the copper wire inside.

Suddenly there was a spark and a flash of light. The truck horn blasted so loud it almost knocked Angelo over on his one ear. He thought the sound would blast his hair off. He felt as if it were going to turn him inside out.

Clarence slapped at the horn button but the horn still blew. He shook the steering wheel, but the sound didn't stop. He stamped on the floor.

Angelo jumped from under the dashboard to the gear shift, and up onto Clarence's shoulder. Clarence made a grab for him, but Angelo jumped back of the seat.

Clarence didn't even have time to yell at Angelo, because he had to give all his attention to the horn. He stopped the truck. He looked up under the dashboard with a flashlight and saw the two gnawed wires that were touching. He pulled the wires apart and the horn stopped.

"It would have served that mouse right if he'd had his head blown off," Clarence muttered. He leaned back in the driver's seat and took a deep breath.

With the truck horn stopped, it was awfully quiet on the mountain. If there's anybody up here to wake up, Clarence thought, that horn sure did wake 'em.

Then he heard another horn. It wasn't the horn of a big rig; it was an automobile horn. It sounded far away, and it came in three short honks, over and over. Clarence knew that three short honks always mean "help."

Somebody's in trouble up here, that's for sure, he thought.

He opened the cab door and climbed down into the snow. He listened. Everything was still with just the wind blowing the snow into deep drifts. Clarence reached up into the cab and pressed the truck horn. It blasted out again. The automobile horn answered with three short honks. The sound was muffled, as if it were under a blanket.

That's not coming from far away, Clarence thought. It's coming out of a snowdrift.

He walked along the road a little way, flashing his light. Then he saw it— a bright spot of yellow in a deep snowdrift.

"It's the school bus," Clarence said out loud, "and it's full of kids!"

He went back to his truck and took out a shovel. The children yelled and cheered while Clarence shoveled snow away from the bus.

The driver was a woman. She climbed out as soon as Clarence could get the door open.

"That truck horn was the sweetest sound I ever heard," the woman driver said. "As soon as I heard it I knew we were safe, because you can always count on a big-rig driver to get you out of trouble."

"Look," Clarence said. "We've got to get you out of here before the snow gets too deep. It looks as if the snowplows might not get up here for a couple of days."

It didn't take Clarence long. He unhooked his trailer full of molasses, backed his tractor up to the school bus, and hooked on a chain. Then he pulled the bus back onto the road.

"Now I'll break a trail through the snow with my rig," Clarence told the driver. "You follow in my tracks and you'll be all right. We're at the summit, and it's all downhill from here on."

Clarence hooked up his trailer again and pushed on past the school bus. The children were all laughing and waving to him. The lady driver was shouting, "Thank you! Thank you!"

Clarence waved back. "Don't thank me, thank my mouse!"

Later, when Clarence had a chance to stop, he found Angelo hiding behind the seat between a monkey wrench and a screw driver. He picked up the mouse and sat him on the dashboard by the windshield.

"Now, mouse," Clarence said, "you and I are partners from here on in. You promise you won't chew up any more wiring, except when somebody needs to be rescued. You promise you won't get into any more cargo, and I'll feed you out of my lunch. I'm going to report this to the company. I'll tell them how you rescued a school bus full of kids, and you'll get a merit award. If you have to chew on something, you can chew on that!"

Now Clarence and Angelo drive the highways, delivering coffee and typewriters, popsicles, dill pickles and electric heaters. They go from one city to another. Angelo has a place to sit by the windshield where he can see the country, and he always has a box of soda crackers to eat. A small card hangs from a knob in the cab:

To Clarence Carter's Mouse, for alertness in rescuing a school bus in a blizzard: permanent and irrevocable rights to ride in the cab of any Company truck.

The card is signed by the President, Traffic Manager, and Dispatcher, and at the bottom it is signed by Clarence Carter, Driver.

THE LONG ROAD TO BOSTON

ELIZABETH COATSWORTH

"You're late," said the woman gathering apples from the trees along the stone wall as they went by.

"You're late," said the man fishing from the bridge.

"You're late," said the farmer who pulled up his team to give them more room.

"You're late," said the old man coming down the steps of the corner store.

"You're late," said the boy driving home the cows

126

from pasture. "The last Thanksgiving turkeys went by a week ago."

It was usually John who explained, "We got held up. Our father was sick." Molly just listened. The words rang in her ears like a bell, over and over, "You're late, you're late."

Father had said the same thing when they started at dawn.

"You're late getting off. I hope you may get there before snow flies or you're likely to lose some of the flock. But don't drive them too hard for they can't stand it. And take care of yourselves."

Mother had run out with a loaf of bread that she had just pulled out of the oven and put it into the pack Molly carried. John, who was older, had the heavier blankets and the three dollars and sixty-five cents. Grandma stood at the door, waving a dishcloth.

"You'll have a beautiful time," she called. "Give my love to Boston."

She didn't say, "You're late." But she was the only one who didn't.

The first day was warm and gentle. There seemed to be no danger in it. John had been to Boston once with Father two or three years ago, but Molly had never been beyond their own valley. When they had climbed the road over the notch, she saw all the world spread out below them in brown and gold woodlands and farms set in emerald-green hay stubble cut in squares. She knew that far to the southeast there lay the great city of Boston and the ocean, but she could scarcely believe that her own eyes could see so much and so far.

"Why, I didn't know the world was like this, John," she said, and he answered in a very grown-up way, "The world is like a lot of things. You'll see."

They went slowly, driving the thirty-four turkeys ahead of them along the grassy edges of the road, so that they might catch crickets and grasshoppers as they went. John took the right-hand side and Molly the left, and with their long switches ending in tufts of leaves they guided the big birds when they strayed.

The turkeys seemed to enjoy themselves. The sun shone along their bronze feathers and the blue and purple-red of the cocks' heads and wattles so that they gleamed like metal. Most of the time they flowed slowly along like a river and Molly would say to herself, looking at the little brook tumbling head over heels beside the road, "We're going downhill to Boston." But sometimes the turkeys would be frightened, or try to go into some field, and then the children had to run to head them off.

Old Turk, the leader, tried to help them. He had been to Boston three times already and knew the road; his calm figure bringing up the procession and the sound of the little bell he wore at his neck steadied the flightier birds. Turk was to come back with them in Samuel Thaxter's wagon after Samuel had unloaded the hams and cheeses he was taking to market.

Sixty miles to go. When a flock started early, they counted on twelve days. But John and Molly were late. It was hard not to urge the turkeys a little. Once or twice, when something scared the flock, John let them run for a while instead of trying to quiet them right away.

"Just that much nearer Boston," he said, as Molly, red-faced and panting, joined him.

"But if they scattered we'd lose a whole lot of time," she said soberly.

"We have to chance it," replied John.

He was fourteen, going on fifteen, and nearly as tall as Father now, although his arms and legs still looked too long for him.

It was John who was in charge. Molly just helped, for she was only eight. John carried the map their father had drawn to show them the road and good places to stop for the night where the turkeys could roost in the orchard. It was John who decided when to let them take dust baths in the ruts of the road, and when to keep them moving.

It was fun that first day. They must have done well, for they came to the first camping place in good time. The map showed a long stretch of woods beyond, so they didn't try to go further, but asked permission of the farmer to camp in the orchard for the night.

"Sure," said the farmer, and his wife said, "You children can bring your blankets and sleep in the kitchen if you like," but John couldn't leave the flock and Molly wouldn't leave him.

"There's an old haystack at the foot of the orchard," the farmer said then. "You'd better sleep in that." But they ate in the kitchen.

"I know how it is," said the man. "I've taken turkeys to Boston in my time. You young ones are pretty late in getting started, aren't you?"

The hay tickled their faces, but it felt warm and soft as they burrowed deep into it. Several times during the night John roused to look at the flock and to make sure that the dark figures roosting among the branches were quiet and safe, but Molly slept all night long, tired out after the excitement of the day.

The second day was as beautiful as the first, and the turkeys seemed in good humor. The heat had brought out the insects and the flock drove the grasshoppers before them in a thin green and brown spray. John coaxed them along and kept them going almost until dusk. He passed the camping place marked on the map and found another nearly three miles further down the road.

This time they were barely given permission to let their turkeys sleep in the orchard. "You kids be careful of your fire," the farmer said. "And don't you use any of my fence rails like one crowd did last year."

"And don't pick any apples either," added his wife. But later she put on her shawl and came down to see how they were getting on.

"I don't know but that you could sleep in the old ice house. It's empty now and the sawdust's dry. And you could keep an eye on your turkeys from there," she said almost grudgingly. As she turned to go she took too small eggs from the pocket of her apron.

"They're only pullet's eggs," she said. "The storekeeper won't take them."

The next day a colder wind blew, and the insects were scarcer. The turkey cocks were more bad-tempered. They spread their tails and gobbled and teetered on their horny feet as they passed people or dogs along the way. But Turk kept on steadily, his little bell ringing, and the children drove the flock along steadily, too.

"Might as well get as far as we can while they're fresh," said John.

That evening they went on until they came to the fourth camping place on their father's map; but they had made the distance in three days, not four.

Molly was tired, although the load on her shoulders grew lighter with every day — it was mostly food she carried. Her feet were sore with walking and her back ached, but she didn't complain.

John helped her build the fire in a corner of the stone wall, but it kept flattening in the wind and almost going out.

"Here," he said, "put a blanket over your shoulders. I'm going to the store to get some feed."

"But it will cost money," Molly quavered.

"I got to do the best I can," John explained. "Those turkeys are getting tuckered a little. I got to feed them."

"If only we weren't the last flock."

"Well, we are and it can't be helped."

Molly sat alone for what seemed to her a long time, with the turkeys roosting about her in the trees. She felt for the first time far away from home and little and lonely. What were the family doing now, she wondered. She didn't seem to care much about Boston. She would have traded Boston and everything in it for a chance to be drying dishes for Mother in the lamplit kitchen at home.

When John came back with the feed in a paper bag, she felt better.

"He let me have it for a quarter," said John, "and I bought us a new loaf of bread for five cents and five cents' worth of rock candy, too."

The rock candy made Molly forget her troubles. And they kept the fire going most of the night and weren't cold either. But the next day it rained and Turk's bell jingled pretty forlornly behind the flock.

The turkeys went well enough, helped on with their morning feed of grain, but the road was muddy and both children were wet to the skin. At noon they ate cold vittles, standing, and by the time they reached the place marked out for the night, they were all glad to stop. It was a drovers' inn, and John sent Molly to ask how much it would cost to put the turkeys into the barn for the night.

A white-haired woman opened the door. "It won't cost you a cent," she said. "But don't tell anyone, or my husband wouldn't like it. He's gone off to Boston and I do as I please. Get the turkeys under cover as soon as you can, boy, and come in. I've got supper ready."

"But we've got some bread and ham still," protested Molly uncertainly.

"Nonsense," the woman replied. "Haven't I had children of my own? Come in and get warm. You look tuckered out."

That night they ate chicken stew and dumplings, hot potatoes, spinach and apple pie, and they slept in feather beds.

"You'll have one good night's rest if I know it," declared the woman. "And if it's rainy tomorrow, you shan't stir one foot."

"But we're late, Ma'am," said John. "We've got to go on, rain or shine, before the snow catches us."

Fortunately the next morning cleared to the north-west, bright and cold. There was a white frost on the ground, but the turkeys didn't seem to mind that.

The woman at the inn had fed the flock as well as the children and would take no money. "All I ask is that you'll stop again next year," she told them. "But don't speak of this if my husband should be here."

All day they traveled well. The road was flattening out now. It was no longer downhill, and the farms and villages were closer together. They dreaded the villages, where the dogs ran out of the yards to bark at the turkeys and the flock scattered. That day they lost their first turkey, a young ₵ock which flew over a couple of board fences and disappeared altogether from sight.

"We can't spend half a day chasing him," John decided after nearly an hour's delay. "Father said we'd never get the whole flock there."

The days grew sharper, and the nights were so cold that John insisted Molly must sleep indoors. She agreed, knowing that he could have double the number of blankets if she weren't there. They made good time and lost no more turkeys, but on the ninth day the air seemed too clear to be trusted.

"It's full moon tonight," said Molly. "Father says look for a change after the full moon."

"If it changes it won't be for rain," muttered John,

and all afternoon he kept his eye on the birds more carefully than ever.

"We've only one more day's trip ahead of us, Molly," he said late in the afternoon, "but if it snows tomorrow maybe we won't be able to get the turkeys through. And if we're delayed for more than a day we won't have any money left. Do you think you could go on walking by moonlight?"

"I could," said Molly stoutly, "but could the turkeys?"

"We'll have to see."

Before dusk John brought food and gave the turkeys all they could eat, while he and Molly had a bigger supper than usual by the side of the road. He wrapped her in blankets and told her to rest until the moon came up. She went to sleep with the turkeys standing uneasily around her. When she woke up, the fire had gone out and the moon had risen, broad and bright in the sky. John wrapped up the blankets and they started off.

Old Turk seemed to understand. He drove the turkeys before him down the moonlit road, his bell twinkling like silver in the light. The other turkeys made complaining noises at first, but after a while they quieted down.

The moonlight was so bright that the road showed brown and the grass had a dark green look in the hayfields. But as the moon rose higher in the sky, a wide ring appeared around it, white and fleecy, and John said, "The moon's wading in snow."

"There're no stars in the ring," said Molly. "That means it'll snow tomorrow."

But in that bright, windless night it seemed as though they were walking in a dream. The turkeys moved as in a dream, too, not running from side to side after grasshoppers, but walking quietly along in the middle of the road to the sound of Turk's little bell. The moonlight flowed whitely from their polished feathers and caught on the buckles of the straps across John's shoulders and the ends of Molly's shoe laces. The lights went out in the houses. All the world lay sleeping but an owl in the woods and a cat hunting along a ditch.

Still the turkeys went on, and the children followed. When the shadows of the buildings and fences and trees lay almost beneath them and the moon in its dark circle was high overhead, and the mist had spread slowly over the sky, John insisted upon a halt.

"But we can go on," Molly argued. "We'd better go on while we're at it."

"No use running a good thing into the ground," declared John. "We're going to eat now and so are the turkeys."

"But you don't have to build a fire!"

"Yes, I do. And you're to sit down now and do as you're told."

Once off her feet, Molly thought she'd never get on them again. John wrapped her up and told her to go to sleep, but he wouldn't rest himself. He heated water over the fire and made a hot bran for the turkeys; then he fed them carefully, seeing that the smaller ones got their share. When all had eaten, he stamped out the fire and wakened Molly.

"Let me alone," she kept saying, "there's no school today," but he kept at her until he roused her at last.

The last half of the night was hard on everyone. Some of the turkeys were limping, and the children had to keep nagging at them.

"That Turk's a wonder," John said, for Turk kept driving the flock ahead as steadily as though he had just started. If John's feet were tired, he never showed it any more than Turk did. But Molly was limping; if she hadn't begun to sing hymns, she might have burst out crying instead. The mist was turning to cloud and the feel of the air had changed. Any country-bred child would have known that snow was coming. The moon was still shining, but in a startled now-you-see-me and now-you-don't way, and the ring around the moon looked like a band of copper.

About four in the morning they reached Cousin Jonathan Cole's house in Cambridge and knocked, though they hated to wake anyone at that hour. John knew the house by the red barn with the weather vane of a horse jumping a fence, and the bow window on the right side of a white door with a round knocker, just as Father had said.

Cousin Jonathan came downstairs with a candle and let them in. Then he put on his clothes and helped John get the turkeys under shelter and fed while Cousin Mattie hurried Molly off to a warm bed.

Neither of the children woke up until noon the next day and it's a wonder that they woke up then, for the light was dimmed by falling snow and the earth was silent under a white blanket already two inches thick. Perhaps it was the smell of Cousin Mattie's good dinner which wakened them.

"My, you do look more like yourselves," said Cousin Mattie cheerfully when they appeared, washed and dressed, at the kitchen door. "You gave me quite a turn when you arrived last night, looking like two ghosts."

"I'd better go see to the turkeys," said John, but Cousin Mattie smiled and shook her head. "Jonathan drove into the market with them this morning in the big cart," she explained. "He's just back and gone out to put up the horses. He got a good price for the turkeys on a late market."

"But he didn't take Turk?" asked Molly anxiously.

"No, he understood about Turk. Turk's out at the barn, smelling about, proud of the trip he's made — and well he may be. No one has ever made such good time with a flock to our knowledge and they brought a better price than they would have last week, when the market was full of turkeys. Lots of folks don't think Thanksgiving's Thanksgiving without a turkey on the platter, but there's a lot will leave it till the last minute. Here's your cousin Jonathan. You'd better all eat a good dinner, for you've lots to do and see before Samuel Thaxter stops to pick you up Monday morning."

THE SNAKE IN THE BOTTLE

RUSSELL DAVIS AND BRENT ASHABRANNER

A king out of the west traveled north and south and east and fought great battles and took much treasure. Since the king was always away at war, he built a great treasure room and hired a man to guard it.

Now the guard of the treasure room was very careful to keep others from stealing the riches of the king. But the guard himself began to steal the king's treasure. For many years the guard took the treasure, little by little, to a storehouse of his own. The guard emptied the chests of gold and silver and jewels and filled them with stones and pebbles.

When the king was old and crippled from his wounds, he returned to his palace to enjoy his treasure. The guard came before the king and said, "Now Your Majesty has returned. There is a lion in the house once more and so no need for an old guard such as I. Who can guard the treasure better than you, my King?"

"You have spoken the truth," the king said. "And you have served me well for many years. Take this great chest of gold and go on your way. Live your remaining days in peace and plenty."

After the guard had gone, the king discovered that his chests were filled with stones and pebbles. The king sent horsemen out to bring back the dishonest guard. The guard tried to escape into another country. But the king's territories had grown very large, and the guard's many mules were heavily laden with gold and treasure. The horsemen found the guard still within the kingdom and spoke to him: "His Majesty bids you return to his palace. He wishes to speak to you."

"Why does he wish to speak to me?" the guard asked. "I have done nothing."

"He has not given us any reason," the soldiers said. "But you must return."

When the guard returned to the palace, the king

told him to sit down in the throne room. "I would like to tell you a very short story," he said. "Once a snake crawled into a farmhouse and found an open jug of milk. The snake crawled in through the narrow neck of the jug and began to drink all of the milk. The snake drank and drank until he was too fat to crawl back through the neck of the jug."

The king stopped speaking and smiled.

"Is that the end of the story?" the guard asked. "I have a long journey and I would like to be off."

"That is not quite the end," the king said. "What must that snake do to get back out of the jug?"

"The snake must spit out the milk," the guard answered.

"True," the king said. "Should he spit out all of it?"

"I think he will have to spit out all of it to get out," the guard said.

"You are very right," the king said. "All of it."

The guard looked up and saw soldiers with spears moving slowly toward him from every door of the throne room.

We can imagine that the guard gave back all of the treasure, just as the king suggested in his little story about the snake trapped in the bottle. It is easy to see why the king did not just order the guard to give back the treasure. Instead the king told a story of a thieving snake. The king wanted to teach the guard a lesson with the story of the snake.

There is no telling whether the guard ever escaped from the throne room, even if he promised to give back the treasure. Like many good stories, "The Snake in the Bottle" leaves the reader with something to think about.

CALICO THE WONDER HORSE
or
THE SAGA OF STEWY SLINKER

VIRGINIA LEE BURTON

Way out West in Cactus County there was a horse named Calico. She wasn't very pretty . . . but she was smart. She was the smartest fastest horse in all of Cactus County. She could run like greased lightning and she could turn on a quarter and give you back fifteen cents in change. She had a long and sensitive nose. She could smell like a real bloodhound. Her nose was keen and she could track a bee through a blizzard.

She belonged to a cowboy whose name was Hank. Hank had saved her from the wolves when she was just a baby colt . . . and Calico never forgot. She would go to the end of the trail for Hank. They had a language all their own and understood each other perfectly.

Everybody was happy and contented in Cactus County. There were no locks, there were no jails, and there were no fences. Twice a year they had a round-up . . . one in the spring and one in the fall. In the spring the cowboys rounded up all the cattle, separated them and branded the new little calves. Hank was top cowpuncher and Calico was top cow-pony.

Across the Cactus River were the Badlands . . . good only for hideouts for Bad Men. Once a month, the stagecoach, driven by Diehard Dan, came over the narrow mountain pass, down the hairpin turns, and forded the river to bring visitors and news from the outside world to the people of Cactus County. One day Diehard Dan brought some bad news.

He had seen Stewy Slinker and his gang of Bad Men . . . Butch Bones, Snake Eye Pyezon, Buzzard Bates and little Skunk Skeeter . . . in the Badlands. Stewy Slinker was said to be so mean he would hold up Santa Claus on Christmas Eve if he had a chance. He rode a horse whose name was Mud. They looked down on Cactus County where there were no fences, no locks and no jail, not even a Deputy Sheriff. They saw the nice fat cattle grazing peacefully on the open range. "Ahaa!" said Stewy Slinker as he curled his long black moustache. "Ahaa!" said he. "Nice pickin's!"

Butch Bones was Stewy Slinker's right-hand man. Butch Bones boasted that he was so tough he would bite a live grizzly bear's nose. Snake Eye Pyezon was Stewy Slinker's left-hand man. He was so crooked, they said, that if he swallowed nails he'd spit out corkscrews. Buzzard Bates was so bad even a buzzard wouldn't use him for bait. Little Skunk Skeeter just tagged along because nobody else liked him.

Stewy Slinker found a good hideout in a cave halfway up a steep mountain. Only a bloodhound could find them there and it would take an army to get them out.

The first dark night they crept quietly down from the Badlands. They rustled a bunch of nice fat cattle from the open range. To cover their trail they drove the cattle into the river and waded upstream before going back to the Badlands.

Near their hideout was a box canyon where they hid the stolen cattle. All summer they rustled cattle from Cactus County. "This is as easy as eating striped candy," said Stewy Slinker, curling both his long black moustaches.

Once again it was round-up time in Cactus County.

Time for the fall round-up when they selected the beef cattle for market. The cowboys rode round and round looking for the cattle. Stewy Slinker and his gang had rustled so many there were few to be found. Stewy Slinker must be caught.

They posted a reward and description of Stewy Slinker. One day when Hank and Calico were reading it . . . Calico had an idea!!!! She told Hank to wait for her, and raced off to the river. She waded up and down the river sniffing right and left till she picked up Stewy Slinker's old cold trail. To disguise herself to look like Stewy Slinker's horse she rolled over and over in the mud on the river bank. Only a bloodhound or *Calico* could have followed Stewy Slinker's trail through the Badlands. Stewy Slinker didn't leave enough tracks to trip an ant.

When Calico reached the hideout she chased Stewy Slinker's horse, Mud, away, then quietly waited outside till Stewy Slinker came out. He mistook her for Mud, saddled her, and got on. Then the fireworks started. Hi! Yi! Whoopee! High went Calico and hard she hit. Calico bounded down the mountainside leaping from rock to rock to rock like a jack-rabbit. Stewy Slinker pulled leather so hard he got calluses on both hands.

Two whoops and a holler and they were over the river. Lightning was slow in comparison to the way they covered the country . . . back to Hank who was waiting. Calico stopped short and unloaded Stewy Slinker who shot through the air like a bullet. He landed in a large patch of cacti. His yells and screams could be heard from one end of Cactus County to the other.

Calico picked Stewy Slinker out of the Cactus Patch. It would take a week to pluck him so he wouldn't look like a porcupine. The people of Cactus County gave Hank and Calico the reward. Hank did not want to take it, but Calico nodded her head and told him she had another good idea. The idea was to give a big party for all the children in Cactus County, to be held in the schoolhouse on Christmas Eve. . . . Everybody was invited.

The next time Diehard Dan came over the mountain pass Hank went back with him to buy the presents.

As there was no jail in Cactus County, Stewy Slinker was put down in the cellar of the schoolhouse with Wishbone Bill to guard him. Through the window Stewy Slinker heard the children talking about the mysterious and precious load that was coming in on the stagecoach. He planned to escape and hold it up. Every night he dug up some dirt and hid it under the bed. In the daytime he covered the hole with his hat. He was digging a tunnel out of the schoolhouse cellar.

The night before the stagecoach was expected he dug the last bit and crawled out. Wishbone Bill didn't see him because he was asleep on his feet. Stewy

Slinker stole Wishbone Bill's horse and hit the trail for the Badlands. To fool anyone who followed him he took to the tall timbers and sent Wishbone Bill's horse on.

"Well, tie my legs in a bowknot," said Wishbone Bill when he woke up and found Stewy Slinker gone. He ran to tell the people. A posse set out on Stewy Slinker's trail. The trail was plain to see. Calico saw the posse go by and she raced after them. When they came to the tall timbers Calico stopped, lifted up her long and sensitive nose, and sniffed . . . but the posse kept right on following the tracks of Wishbone Bill's horse.

When Stewy Slinker reached the hideout he told his men of the mysterious and precious load coming in on the stagecoach and his plans to hold it up. Calico, hot on the trail of Stewy Slinker, got there just in time to hear the plan. She had another idea.

Meanwhile back in Cactus County, everybody from the oldest to the youngest had turned out for the party at the schoolhouse. (Everybody but the posse who were still out looking for Stewy Slinker.) They came in their best Sunday-go-to-meetin'-clothes, in buggies, in buckboards, and in wagons. For weeks the women-folks had been baking cakes and pies and doughnuts. Hank off in the city had bought hundreds of presents for the children. The stagecoach was loaded high. They got started late and knew they would have to hurry. As they neared the Badlands the sky grew blacker and blacker. Diehard Dan cracked his whip and said, "Looks like a real goose-drownder. We better get out of these mountains and across that river before she breaks or we'll have to wait a week."

Meanwhile Calico had found the box canyon filled with the stolen cattle. She let down the gate. Just then there was a blinding flash of lightning. The cattle had been restless before. The lightning was all that was needed to start a stampede. Calico led the way.

Stewy Slinker and his gang were waiting at the narrow mountain pass. "Here she comes!" said Stewy Slinker. "Take your places, but hold your fire till I give the word. On your marks! Get set! Fire!" Bing! Bang! Shing! Zing! Off went Hank's hat with a hole in it. Off went Diehard Dan's hat with another hole in it. "Whoaa!" said Diehard Dan. "Reach for the sky!" said Stewy Slinker: and Hank and Diehard Dan reached. "I wish Calico were here," said Hank.

"Look!" yelled Skunk Skeeter.

It was Calico at the head of the stampede. "Run for your lives! Quick! Inside the stagecoach or you'll be trampled to death!" yelled Stewy Slinker.

Stewy Slinker grabbed the reins from Diehard Dan. "Giddyap!" and they were off.

"Come on! Calico!" called Hank. As Calico drew near, Hank leaped from the stagecoach to her back. Stewy Slinker drove the stagecoach down the narrow mountain road at a breakneck speed. Hank and Calico were fast behind and the stampede thundering after them.

Inside the stagecoach Snake Eye Pyezon said, "Whew! That was so close a shave I nearly lost my whiskers."

Faster and faster they went. The Bad Men inside the stagecoach were being shaken around like dry peas in a pod. Bop! Bang! Bump! Crack! "Ouch! My head!" wailed Butch Bones as he hit the roof. "Ouch! My nose!" cried Buzzard Bates. Poor little Skunk Skeeter couldn't say anything because he was underneath them all.

Faster and faster they raced. There was a sharp turn ahead. Stewy Slinker reached for the brake . . . too late! One wheel went over the edge. Diehard Dan, on the near side, leapt to safety. Then . . . over they went!

Hank and Calico saw them go and slid down the mountainside to look for them. They found Stewy Slinker hanging up in a tree by his gun belt. Hank took the gun and unhooked him. The stagecoach and horses had landed safely . . . without a scratch. But the rest of the Bad Men were nowhere in sight. Hank went to the door of the stagecoach and said, "Hands up!" . . . No answer. He opened the door. There they were . . . and a sad looking sight too.

Hank put Stewy Slinker inside with his Bad Men

and collected all the guns. Diehard Dan got the stage-coach back on the road again.

Then the cloudburst burst! ! ! It rained so hard and so fast that if you opened your mouth you'd be in danger of drowning. The cattle slowed down and safely crossed the river. Stewy Slinker looked out the window at the rain and laughed to himself. Heh! Heh! We're not caught yet. That river will be flooded in a few minutes and no one can cross it for days. Hank and Calico knew it too. There was one chance that they could make it and they must take that chance. They left the road, skipped the hairpin turns, and slid straight down the mountain. At the edge of the river the stagecoach horses were frightened and re-fused to cross. Hank grabbed the lead horse reins and pulled them in. Closer and closer came the wall of raging water. . . . Higher and higher rose the river. . . . Hurry!

They just made it and raced on to the schoolhouse. On the way they passed the cattle grazing peacefully on the home range. The storm was over. The moon came out. It was a beautiful night.

When they got to the schoolhouse the children ran out to greet them and danced around Hank and Calico. "What shall I do with the Bad Men?" said Hank to Calico. Calico had another good idea. "Come on, boys," said Hank, taking Calico's advice. "This is Christmas Eve. Everybody is invited to the party.

You too." The Bad Men were bashful. Hank loaded them up with presents and the children pulled them inside . . . all but Stewy Slinker. He sneaked out the other door of the stagecoach and peeked in the window. He saw what the mysterious and precious load was. He felt very sad. So sad that he sat down and cried. "I didn't know I was that mean . . . holding up Santa Claus on Christmas Eve. I'm never going to be bad any more."

Calico found him and persuaded him to go inside to join the others. Everybody was having a good time, even Stewy Slinker. He sat down on the floor and showed young Wishbone Bill how to run his new toy train. Buzzard Bates got hit on the nose by a jack-in-the-box and laughed and laughed. Butch Bones pretended he was a grizzly bear and let the children ride on his back. Snake Eye Pyezon played dolls and Skunk Skeeter had the time of his life because everybody liked him. When the posse got back and found the Bad Men playing with toys on the floor with the children, they could hardly believe their eyes.

Everybody had such a good time at the party that it lasted till New Year's Day, and then the Bad Men promised to be good. Hank was elected Sheriff of Cactus County and Calico was made his Deputy Sheriff. They all shook hands and once again everybody was happy and contented in Cactus County.

MR. DAWSON FLIES A KITE

R. O. WORK

One day Mrs. Dawson said, "Donald, you promised to clean the fruit cellar for me today. I have a lot of canning to put away and I want the cellar cleaned first."

"I was just going to start it, Marjorie," said Mr. Dawson. "But I must return this screw driver to Mr. Long first. I'll do it as soon as I get back."

On his way home from the Longs' house Mr. Dawson saw one of the Slow boys flying a kite.

"Good afternoon," said Mr. Dawson. "Which one of the boys are you?"

"I'm Robert," the boy said. "Look how high my kite is."

"Is that a message tied to the string?" asked Mr. Dawson. "I used to do that when I was a boy. I like to fly kites."

"All great men like to fly kites," said Robert. "Benjamin Franklin flew a kite. I read about it at school. He put a key on his."

"A key?" said Mr. Dawson. "Why did he do that?"

"He found out something but I've forgotten what. I wanted to put a key on mine but we haven't any keys."

"I wonder what he found out?" said Mr. Dawson, and he looked thoughtful. "Robert, we have a key for our fruit cellar. Do you suppose if I put that on we'd find out what Benjamin Franklin did?"

"I don't know," answered Robert. "We could try."

Robert reeled in his kite, and he and Mr. Dawson went to get the key to the fruit cellar.

"I'd better turn this key," said Mr. Dawson, "just in case Marjorie wants to get into the fruit cellar while we're gone."

Mr. Dawson tied the key on the string and Robert

ran with his kite. "There she goes, Mr. Dawson!" he shouted. "She's really climbing now."

"Let me hold the string for a while," said Mr. Dawson.

"Well, all right," agreed Robert, "but don't let it out too fast or she'll dive."

"Oh, I've flown lots of kites," said Mr. Dawson. "I know how to handle them."

He let the string out slowly and the kite climbed higher and higher in the air. "You can hardly see the key now," said Robert. "I wish I could remember what is supposed to happen."

Just then Mrs. Slow could be heard calling the children to supper. "Oh, golly," cried Robert. "I'll be late for supper again if I don't go now and it'll take a long time to get my kite down."

"You run along, Robert," said Mr. Dawson. "I'll take your kite down for you."

Robert went home for supper and Mr. Dawson started to reel in the kite. He had it almost in when the ball of string slipped from his hands and rolled along the ground. The wind caught the kite and it soared upward again.

Mr. Dawson tried to catch the string but he was too late. The kite swooped first to the left and then to the right. It spun around in the air for a minute and then dived to the ground. Mr. Dawson closed his eyes tight. "Oh dear," he said, "I hope it misses the trees."

But when he opened his eyes the kite was dangling from the top of an oak tree. The string was all tangled in the branches. "My word," he thought, "however am I going to get that kite down for Robert?" He thought of climbing up after it, but the tree was a tall one and the kite was at the very top.

"I hope Robert won't be too disappointed," he thought. "Perhaps I can make him another kite tomorrow."

When Mr. Dawson got home, Mrs. Dawson was nowhere around. "Marjorie, oh, Marjorie!" he called. But there was no answer. He looked all over the house but he couldn't find her. "Where in the world can she be?" he said. "It's after suppertime now. She's always here at suppertime. Perhaps she's at the Longs'."

Mr. Dawson called the Longs' house. "Good evening, Mrs. Long. Marjorie isn't home. I was wondering if she was at your house."

Just then Mr. Dawson thought he heard a knock at the back door. "Just a minute, please, Mrs. Long. There's someone at the back door."

But when Mr. Dawson opened the door there was no one there. "That's strange," he thought, "I was sure I heard someone knocking." He went back to the telephone. "Is she there, Mrs. Long?"

"No, Mr. Dawson," said Mrs. Long. "I haven't seen her all day. Have you telephoned Mrs. Short?"

"No, I haven't," said Mr. Dawson. "I'll call there now. Thank you, Mrs. Long."

Mr. Dawson called the Shorts' number. "She isn't here," said Mrs. Short.

"Oh, just a minute, Mrs. Short. There's someone at the back door." But again when Mr. Dawson opened the door no one was there. He went back to the telephone.

"I haven't seen her all day," said Mrs. Short. "Have you tried the Blacks'?"

Mr. Dawson called the Blacks' but she wasn't there. She wasn't at the Whites' or at the Greens', and there was still no one at the back door although Mr. Dawson had answered it each time he heard the knocking.

"She must be visiting with Mrs. Blue," said Mr. Dawson. "I'll call there. Oh, dear, there's that knocking again!"

"No," said Mrs. Blue when he called her, "I haven't seen her all day and it's pretty late. I wonder what could have happened to her?"

"I don't know," said Mr. Dawson, "but there's something mighty funny going on here. Someone keeps knocking at the back door. I've answered it five times now but there's no one there."

"Goodness gracious," said Mrs. Blue. "I'll tell Mr.

Blue and he and some of the other men will come over and help you. I do hope nothing dreadful has happened."

It didn't take Mr. Blue and the other men long to reach Mr. Dawson's house. They came into the kitchen with worried looks on their faces. "When did you see Mrs. Dawson last, Donald?" asked Mr. Green.

"It was right after lunch," said Mr. Dawson. "I left her in the kitchen canning tomatoes when I went to Mr. Long's house to return his screw driver. On the way home I met Robert Slow and he was — Listen! Wasn't that a knock at the back door?"

"Sounded more as though it came from downstairs," said Mr. Black. "Let's go have a look."

The men all went into the basement but everything seemed to be in order there. They had just started upstairs when they heard the knocking again. It was louder now.

"It sounds as though it's coming from the fruit cellar," said Mr. Black. "Hello!" he called loudly.

"Hello," came the answer. "Please let me out of here."

"Great Scot! It's Marjorie," said Mr. Dawson. "Oh, Marjorie, I've been so worried about you. Come upstairs now. It's late."

"I can't," said Mrs. Dawson. "I can't get out."

"Oh, my word!" gasped Mr. Dawson.

"What's the matter, Donald?" asked Mr. Short.

"The key. It's at the top of the oak tree by the pasture fence."

"What in the world is it doing there?" asked Mr. Long.

"Well, you see, Robert . . . oh, it's a very long story, Mr. Long, and it's all mixed up with Benjamin Franklin. I haven't time to tell you now. We'll have to get that key right away."

The men took ladders and flashlights and went out to the oak tree where the kite was. It took more than an hour to get the key, but finally they got it down and Robert's kite too. Mr. Dawson was very grateful. "I don't know how I'd have managed it without help," he said. "Thank you very much."

He was starting home when Mr. Slow arrived. "Good evening," he said. "Has Mrs. Dawson been found yet?"

"Oh, yes, thank you, Mr. Slow," said Mr. Dawson, "and here's Robert's kite. I told him I'd take care of it for him."

"Thank you, Mr. Dawson," said Mr. Slow. "It was nice of you to remember it."

Mrs. Dawson was very glad to get out of the fruit cellar. "I was putting away the tomatoes I canned," she said, "and then I couldn't get out of the fruit cellar. I can't imagine what happened. I guess the lock must have caught somehow."

"Oh, Marjorie, I'm so sorry that happened," said Mr. Dawson. "It must have frightened you."

"Not at all, Donald," said Mrs. Dawson. "I didn't mind a bit and I got the fruit cellar all cleaned so you won't have to do it after all."

That night after Mr. Dawson was in bed, he said, "Marjorie, why do suppose Benjamin Franklin tied a key to his kite string?"

"That's how he found out about electricity," said Mrs. Dawson. "Why?"

But Mr. Dawson had already fallen asleep and didn't even hear her.

A HERO BY MISTAKE

by

ANITA BRENNER

There was once a man named Dionisio who was very much afraid. He happened to be an Indian.

Grown men of course are not supposed to be afraid, and especially not Indians. Who ever heard of a frightened Indian?

This Dionisio lived in a hut near the woods, in Mexico. He was a Mexican Indian.

He had a few neighbors who lived in a village near him. Others were scattered around the valley in huts

like his own, except some huts were bigger because
their owners were rich.

There were also the mountains. They made Dionisio
feel very safe, because they were so big and lovely
and peaceful. But when he was afraid, even the mountains seemed dark and full of evil things.

Sometimes it seemed as if almost anything made
him feel uuuuh!, and like rocks inside him, and like
running away and hiding all at once. You know
how it is.

For instance, one morning he felt something behind him. A shape! Something following him! He
began to run. The shape ran too. He saw it running
and he ran harder, and the more he ran the more
afraid he was . . . and this shape right behind him.

Yes, of course, it was his own shadow. Dionisio
realized it when he had to stop for breath.

"Oh what a silly I am!" he said, and hit himself on
the head with his two hands.

The people who lived in the village all knew that
Dionisio was not a brave man. Sometimes he was so
afraid he ran lickety-split like a cat, and they laughed
at him.

And afterwards he would laugh too, and say, "How
silly!" Then there was a happy feeling for "there is
nothing so much, after all, to be afraid of in this
world."

Dionisio was a wood-chopper. Once he was chopping up on the mountain, and heard another axe far away. Another wood-cutter he thought, and yelled, "I'm Dionisio!"

A far-away hoarse voice answered:

DIONISIO

"He knows me." And he began to worry, "I'm alone here," and . . . "what if he isn't my friend?"

He worried and wondered and wondered and worried, then he yelled "Who are you? Friend or enemy . . .?" The voice came back very shrill, ". . . ENEMY!"

"Oh, dear," Dionisio thought, "I've just got to be brave." So he shouted fiercely, "If you bother me I'll kill you!" And the voice yelled even more ferociously, "I'll kill you . . . !"

And then Dionisio, terrified, began to run. He ran to the village for help.

So ten brave men came back with him. At the place where Dionisio had heard the ferocious voice they started to yell, and ten brave voices yelled right back. Then they laughed and laughed because, of course, it was just an echo. "Oh what a silly I am!" said Dionisio and hit himself on the head and laughed like anything, too.

Dionisio was a frightened man all right, but he was a hard worker. He worked so hard that finally he had chopped all the wood the people in his valley needed, and so nobody would buy any more.

So, Dionisio loaded his burro and went out to look

for a market. He traveled and traveled until way ahead there, he saw a town. When he was almost there, "Crash! Crash! Crash!" he heard.

"Oh me, oh my" said Dionisio, "Shooting!"

How could he run away and leave his burro?

"Crash! Crash! Crash!"

So Dionisio got under his burro. There he was, shaking and trembling, when along the road came a little old woman. She was surprised to see a man all curled up in a ball under his burro.

"What are you doing there, good neighbor?" the old woman asked. "Are you ill?"

"Oh madam," Dionisio said to her because he was a good-natured man, "you'd better get under here too. You might be killed."

"But who would kill us, good sir? We're all peaceful folks here," she said.

"Who knows what black souls are shooting up the town," Dionisio said. "Come quickly, before you're killed!"

Then the old woman began to laugh. "Oh, goodness," she said, laughing and laughing, "it's firecrackers."

"Firecrackers? But what for? It isn't a holiday today!"

"Well, it is here. It's the christening of the baby daughter of Don Gedovius. Oh poor you," said the old lady, laughing like anything. "How frightened you must have been. Come on out now, you look very strange under that burro."

"Oh," said Dionisio hitting himself on the head, "but . . . what a silly I am!"

Now, you can't sell wood in a town where everybody is busy celebrating, so Dionisio went on. After a while he met a man who had musical instruments for sale: guitars, violins, and bugles.

He was so pleased that nothing had happened to him that he bought a bugle, and the man taught him then and there to play it, "ta-ta-ta-ta-ta-ta-ta-taaaaaa!" the way soldiers blow.

So along went Dionisio again with his bugle and his burrow and all the load of wood that he wanted to sell. Pretty soon there were more wheel tracks in the road.

He was near another town, when again, of all things, he heard "Crash! Crash!" And louder, "CRASH-CRASH-CRASH!"

"This time," Dionisio said to himself, "I'm not going to be such a silly. I shall blow my bugle so I'll be invited to the party. I'm getting very hungry, and certainly where there's a christening there ought to be a turkey dinner." And, happily, Dionisio blew his bugle the way the soldiers do.

And what do you think? Five men on horseback galloped cloppity-clop furiously out of the town, in a great big cloud of dust. They had handkerchiefs tied around their faces.

"And who would they be?" Dionisio thought as he watched them disappear down the road. "They certainly need those handkerchiefs around their noses, in all that dust."

He was still standing looking at the dust when a lot of people came running out of town — men, women, and children. They hugged him and said, "Oh sir, you have saved us!"

"Me?" said Dionisio. "But from what?"

"Why, from those bad men who rode in on horseback and wanted to rob us! When you blew your bugle they thought it was soldiers — we all thought so — and how they ran!"

"What a brave man you are!"

"Me?" said Dionisio.

Well, they just had to give him a party. They wouldn't take no for an answer.

And they gave him so many presents he could hardly get them all loaded onto his burro.

It was night-time when he said goodbye . . . and no way to tell them he was afraid to leave . . . that he was such a frightened man he had never gone anywhere alone at night.

So there went Dionisio along the dark road, holding on to his burro and feeling like rocks in his stomach, he was so afraid. Suddenly, ahead of him he saw two great big glowing eyes, coming toward him, fast.

They came along closer and closer. "Help! Help! Save me from this monster!" yelled Dionisio and jumped into the bushes pulling his burro after him.

Then whoooosh! Something raced past in a flood of light. The monster was just a truck.

"Oh, my," said Dionisio. "Silly, silly, me!"

And so, sillying himself along, he reached the dirt road to his village. He was going up a slope, very pleased to be so near home, when almost right ahead of him he saw two lights that looked like eyes, again. They were smaller than the others had been, and they glowed in a very ugly way.

"I'm not going to be such a silly this time," said Dionisio sternly to himself, and kept straight on.

But then his burro wouldn't budge. He planted his forelegs stiff and just would not go on, and shook as if frightened.

"Arreh! Giddyap, giddyap. Arreh!" Dionisio scolded and tugged and pulled. But the burro, instead of going forward, started to back up.

Dionisio was so busy struggling with his animal that he forgot about the ugly lights on the road, and then whish! something jumped.

It was a wildcat! Dionisio saw it scrambling away among the bushes, running from him.

"Then wildcats are afraid, too?" Dionisio marveled. "How strange. A wildcat afraid of me!"

He was still thinking about that when he got home and lay down to sleep.

He was fast asleep when suddenly he awoke. There seemed to be something making a noise. Something outside. Walking softly, softly.

"Oh dear!" said Dionisio. "Some robber surely saw me leave that town all loaded with presents and followed me. And here, sure enough, is the end of me."

He didn't know what to do. He just rolled up in a little ball in a corner of his hut, shaking and trembling so hard his teeth went tat-tat in his head.

Then he heard those steps again, closer. Softly, softly, the door was being pushed open.

He couldn't stand it then. He jumped up and yelled. And what does he see!

His burro, that had gotten loose from its stall!

"Oh," said Dionisio, "is there anyone in the whole world like me? What a silly I am!" And he hit himself on the head like anything, and went back to sleep.

A little while later, he woke up again. Again he heard softly, softly, something moving around out there. Like steps.

"Oh you stupid burro!" Dionisio yelled. "Wait till you see what I'll do to you, waking me up like that!"

And he jumped up and grabbed his lasso and rushed out.

Outside everything was dark. All he could see was something running in the dark near the cactus patch. So he grabbed a hunk of firewood and threw it as hard as he could, he was so angry.

"That will teach you to run away."

Then, gripping his lasso, he ran to the cactus patch. He was running hard when he tripped over something big and soft and almost fell over it.

He looked to see what it was and it was a man, fallen among the cactus, unconscious and bleeding. Dionisio had hit him square on the head when he threw that wood.

Well, naturally, Dionisio tied him up. Then he went to call the authorities to come and see who that man was and find out what he was doing in Dionisio's cactus patch.

So the authorities came to look into this matter. And they took the man away.

And the next day, a telegram arrives. It says that there is a very wicked and dangerous man in the neighborhood, that there's fifty thousand pesos for whoever brings him in, and sixty thousand if they bring him in alive.

"Uuum," said the authorities. "Wonder if that is the fellow Dionisio caught?"

And he was. He was the very same bandit that they

were searching for. So they gave Dionisio the sixty thousand. The municipal president made a speech, and the band played a victory march.

From then on, Dionisio wasn't called Dionisio any more. As he was rich, everybody called him Don Dionisio, which is the same as, respectfully, Mister.

And every time he said, "Oh, what a silly I am!" they all said to him, "Oh no, sir, you are the most intelligent and bravest man in the whole region. You are a hero!"

And did Don Dionisio get over being afraid? The truth is, he didn't. Only, since people said he was brave, he acted brave, and somehow or other that made him feel so.

The thing that Dionisio didn't know was that he really was brave.

How can you be brave when you are afraid? Well, if you do what you are afraid to do, that is brave. That is the bravest thing there is, as a matter of fact. And so Dionisio, the frightened Indian, really became what people believed him to be: a very, very brave man.

THE HUNDRED DRESSES

ELEANOR ESTES

Today, Monday, Wanda Petronski was not in her seat. But nobody, not even Peggy and Madeline, the girls who started all the fun, noticed her absence. Usually Wanda sat in the next to the last seat in the last row in Room Thirteen. She sat in the corner of the room where the rough boys who did not make good marks on their report cards sat; the corner of the room where there was most scuffling of feet, most roars of laughter when anything funny was said, and most mud and dirt on the floor.

Wanda did not sit there because she was rough and noisy. On the contrary, she was very quiet and rarely said anything at all. And nobody had ever heard her laugh out loud. Sometimes she twisted her mouth into a crooked sort of smile, but that was all.

Nobody knew exactly why Wanda sat in that seat, unless it was because she came all the way from Boggins Heights and her feet were usually caked with dry mud. Maybe the teacher liked to keep all the children with dirty shoes in one corner of the room. But no one really thought much about Wanda Petronski, once she was in the classroom.

The time when they thought about Wanda was outside of school hours— at noontime when they were coming back to school, or in the morning early before school began, when groups of two or three, or even more, would be talking and laughing on their way to the schoolyard.

Then, sometimes, they waited for Wanda — to have fun with her.

The next day, Tuesday, Wanda was not in school, either. And nobody noticed her absence again, except the teacher, and probably big Bill Byron, who sat in the seat behind Wanda's and who could now put his long legs around her empty desk, one on each side, and sit there like a frog, to the great entertainment of all in his corner of the room.

But on Wednesday, Peggy and Maddie, who sat down front with other children who got good marks and who didn't track in a whole lot of mud, did notice that Wanda wasn't there. Peggy was the most popular girl in school. She was pretty; she had many pretty clothes, and her auburn hair was curly. Maddie was her closest friend.

The reason Peggy and Maddie noticed Wanda's absence was because Wanda had made them late to school. They had waited and waited for Wanda, to have some fun with her, and she just hadn't come.

They often waited for Wanda Petronski — to have fun with her.

Wanda Petronski. Most of the children in Room Thirteen didn't have names like that. They had names easy to say, like Thomas, Smith, or Allen. There was one boy named Bounce, Willie Bounce, and people thought that was funny, but not funny in the same way that Petronski was.

Wanda didn't have any friends. She came to school alone and went home alone. She always wore a faded blue dress that didn't hang right. It was clean, but it looked as though it had never been ironed properly. She didn't have any friends, but a lot of girls talked to her. Sometimes, they surrounded her in the schoolyard as she stood watching the little girls play hop-scotch on the worn hard ground.

"Wanda," Peggy would say in a most courteous manner, as though she were talking to Miss Mason or to the principal. "Wanda," she'd say, giving one of her friends a nudge, "tell us. How many dresses did you say you had hanging up in your closet?"

"A hundred," Wanda said.

"A hundred!" exclaimed all the little girls incredu-lously, and they would stop playing hopscotch and listen.

"Yeah, a hundred, all lined up," said Wanda. Then her thin lips drew together in silence.

"What are they like? All silk, I bet," said Peggy.

"Yeah, all silk, all colors."

"Velvet, too?"

"Yeah, velvet too. A hundred dresses," Wanda would repeat stolidly. "All lined up in my closet."

Then they'd let her go. And then before she'd gone very far, they couldn't help bursting into shrieks and peals of laughter.

A hundred dresses! Obviously, the only dress Wanda had was the blue one she wore every day. So why did she say she had a hundred? What a story! And the girls laughed derisively while Wanda moved over to the sunny place by the ivy-covered brick wall of the school building where she usually stood and waited for the bell to ring.

But if the girls had met her at the corner of Oliver Street, they'd walk along with her for a way, stopping every few feet for more incredulous questions.

"How many shoes did you say you had?"

"Sixty."

"Sixty! Sixty pairs or sixty shoes?"

"Sixty pairs. All lined up in my closet."

"Yesterday, you said fifty."

"Now, I got sixty."

Cries of exaggerated politeness greeted this.

"All alike?"

"Oh, no. Every pair is different. All colors. All lined up." And Wanda would shift her eyes quietly from Peggy to a distant spot as though she were looking far ahead, looking but not seeing anything.

Then the outer fringe of the crowd of girls would break away gradually, laughing, and little by little in pairs the group would disperse. Peggy, who had thought up this game, and Maddie, her inseparable friend, were always the last to leave. Finally Wanda would move up the street, her eyes dull and her mouth closed, hitching her left shoulder every now and then in the funny way she had, finishing the walk to school alone.

Peggy was not really cruel. She protected small children from bullies. And she cried for hours if she saw an animal mistreated. If anybody had said to her, "Don't you think that is a cruel way to treat Wanda?"

she would have been very surprised. Cruel? Why did the girl say she had a hundred dresses? Anybody could tell that that was a lie. Why did she want to lie? And she wasn't just an ordinary person, else why did she have a name like that? Anyway, they never made her cry.

As for Maddie, this business of asking Wanda every day how many dresses and how many hats, and how many this and that she had was bothering her. Maddie was poor herself. She usually wore somebody's hand-me-down clothes. Thank goodness, she didn't live up on Boggins Heights or have a funny name. And her forehead didn't shine the way Wanda's did.

Sometimes, when Peggy was asking Wanda those questions in that mocking polite voice, Maddie felt embarrassed and studied the marbles in the palm of her hand, rolling them around, and saying nothing herself. She would never have paid any attention to Wanda if Peggy hadn't invented the dresses game. But suppose Peggy and all the others started in on her next? She wasn't as poor as Wanda, perhaps, but she was poor. Of course she would have more sense than to say she had a hundred dresses. Still she would not like for them to begin on her. She wished Peggy would stop teasing Wanda Petronski.

Today, even though they had been late to school, Maddie was glad she had not had to make fun of Wanda. She worked her arithmetic problems absentmindedly. "Eight times eight — let's see . . ." She wished she had the nerve to write Peggy a note, because she knew she never would have the courage to speak right out to Peggy, to say, "Hey, Peg, let's stop asking Wanda how many dresses she has." When she finished her arithmetic she did start a note to Peggy. Suddenly she paused and shuddered. She pictured herself in the schoolyard, a new target for Peggy and the girls. Peggy might ask her where she got the dress that she had on, and Maddie would have to say that it was one of Peggy's old ones that Maddie's mother had tried to disguise with new trimmings so that no one in Room Thirteen would recognize it.

If only Peggy would decide of her own accord to stop having fun with Wanda. Oh, well! Maddie ran her hand through her short blonde hair as though to push the uncomfortable thoughts away. What difference did it make? Slowly Maddie tore into bits the note she had started. She was Peggy's best friend, and Peggy was the best-liked girl in the whole room. Peggy could not possibly do anything that was really wrong, she thought.

As for Wanda, she was just some girl who lived up on Boggins Heights and stood alone in the schoolyard. She scarcely ever said anything to anybody. The only time she talked was in the schoolyard about her hundred dresses. Maddie once remembered her telling about one of her dresses, a pale blue one, with cerise-colored trimmings. And she remembered another that was brilliant jungle green, with a red sash. "You'd look like a Christmas tree in that," the girls had said in pretended admiration.

Thinking about Wanda and her hundred dresses all lined up in the closet, Maddie began to wonder who was going to win the drawing and color contest. For girls, this contest consisted of designing dresses, and for boys, of designing motor boats. Probably Peggy would win the girls' medal. Peggy drew better than any one else in the room. At least, that's what everybody thought. She could copy a picture in a magazine or some film star's head so that you could almost tell who it was. Oh, Maddie was sure Peggy would win. Well, tomorrow the teacher was going to announce the winners. Then they'd know.

The next day it was drizzling. Maddie and Peggy hurried to school under Peggy's umbrella. Naturally, on a day like this, they didn't wait for Wanda Petronski on the corner of Oliver Street, the street that far, far away, under the railroad tracks and up the hill, led to Boggins Heights. Anyway, they weren't taking chances on being late today, because today was important.

"Do you think Miss Mason will surely announce the winners today?" asked Peggy.

"Oh, I hope so, the minute we get in," said Maddie. She added, "Of course, you'll win, Peg."

"Hope so," said Peggy eagerly.

The minute they entered the classroom, they stopped short and gasped. There were drawings all over the room, on every ledge and window sill, dazzling colors and brilliant, lavish designs, all drawn on great sheets of wrapping paper. There must have been a hundred of them all lined up.

These must be the drawings for the contest. They were! Everybody stopped and whistled or murmured admiringly.

As soon as the class had assembled, Miss Mason announced the winners. Jack Beggles had won for the boys, she said and his design for an outboard motor was on exhibition in Room Twelve, along with the sketches by all the other boys.

"As for the girls," she said, "although just one or two sketches were submitted by most, one girl — and Room Thirteen should be proud of her — this one girl actually drew one hundred designs — all different and all beautiful. In the opinion of the judges, any one of the drawings is worthy of winning the prize. I am very happy to say that Wanda Petronski is the winner of the girls' medal. Unfortunately, Wanda has been absent from school for some days and is not here to receive the applause that is due her. Let us hope she will be back tomorrow. Now, class, you may file around the room quietly and look at her exquisite drawings."

The children burst into applause, and even the boys were glad to have a chance to stamp on the floor, put their fingers in their mouths and whistle, though they were not interested in dresses.

"Look, Peg," whispered Maddie. "There's that blue one she told us about. Isn't it beautiful?"

"Yes," said Peggy. "And here's that green one. Boy, and I thought I could draw."

While the class was circling the room, the monitor from the principal's office brought Miss Mason a note. Miss Mason read it several times and studied it thoughtfully for a while. Then she clapped her hands.

"Attention, class. Everyone back to his seat."

When the shuffling of feet had stopped and the room was still and quiet, Miss Mason said, "I have a letter from Wanda's father that I want to read to you."

Miss Mason stood there a moment and the silence in the room grew tense and expectant. The teacher adjusted her glasses slowly and deliberately. Her manner indicated that what was coming — this letter from Wanda's father — was a matter of great importance. Everybody listened closely as Miss Mason read the brief note.

Dear Teacher:
My Wanda will not come to your school any more. Jake also. Now we move away to big city.

No more holler "Polack." No more ask why funny name. Plenty of funny names in the big city.

Yours truly,

Jan Petronski

A deep silence met the reading of this letter. Miss Mason took off her glasses, blew on them, and wiped them on her soft white handkerchief. Then she put them on again, and looked at the class. When she spoke her voice was very low.

"I am sure that none of the boys and girls in Room Thirteen would purposely and deliberately hurt anyone's feelings because his name happened to be a long, unfamiliar one. I prefer to think that what was said was said in thoughtlessness. I know that all of you feel the way I do, that this is a very unfortunate thing to have happen — unfortunate and sad, both. And I want you all to think about it."

The first period was a study period. Maddie tried to prepare her lessons, but she could not put her mind on her work. She had a very sick feeling in the bottom of her stomach. True, she had not enjoyed listening to Peggy ask Wanda how many dresses she had in her closet, but she had said nothing. She had stood by silently, and that was just as bad as what Peggy had done. Worse. She was a coward. At least, Peggy hadn't considered they were being mean, but she, Maddie, had thought they were doing wrong. She could put herself in Wanda's shoes. But she had done just as much as Peggy to make life miserable for Wanda by simply standing by and saying nothing. She had helped to make someone so unhappy that she had had to move away from town.

Goodness! Wasn't there anything she could do? If only she could tell Wanda she hadn't meant to hurt her feelings. She turned around and stole a glance at Peggy, but Peggy did not look up. She seemed to be studying hard. Well, whether Peggy felt badly or not, she, Maddie, had to do something. She had to find Wanda Petronski. Maybe she had not yet moved away. Maybe Peggy would climb the Heights with her, and they would tell Wanda she had won the contest, that they thought she was smart and the hundred dresses were beautiful.

When school was dismissed in the afternoon, Peggy said, with pretended casualness, "Hey, let's go and see if that kid has left town or not."

So Peggy had had the same idea! Maddie glowed. Peg was really all right.

The two girls hurried out of the building, up the street toward Boggins Heights, the part of town that wore such a forbidding air on this kind of November afternoon, drizzly, damp and dismal.

"Well, at least," said Peggy gruffly, "I never did call her a foreigner or make fun of her name. I never thought she had the sense to know we were making fun of her anyway. I thought she was too dumb. And gee, look how she can draw!"

Maddie could say nothing. All she hoped was that they would find Wanda. She wanted to tell her that they were sorry they had picked on her, and how wonderful the whole school thought she was, and — please, not to move away and everybody would be nice. She and Peggy would fight anybody who was not nice. Maddie fell to imagining a story in which she and Peggy assailed any bully who might be going to pick on Wanda. "Petronski Onski!" somebody would yell, and she and Peggy would pounce on the guilty one. For a time Maddie consoled herself with these thoughts, but they soon vanished, and again she felt unhappy and wished everything could be nice the way it was before any of them had made fun of Wanda.

Br-r-r. How drab and cold and cheerless it was up here on the Heights! In the summer time, the trees, the sumac, and the ferns that grew along the brook on the side of the road made this a beautiful walk on Sunday afternoons. But now it did not seem beautiful. The brook had dried up. And today's drizzle just sharpened the outline of the rusty tin cans, old shoes, and the forlorn remnants of a big black umbrella in the bed of the brook.

The two girls hurried on. They hoped to get to the top of the hill before dark. Otherwise, they were not certain they could find Wanda's house. At last, puffing and panting, they rounded the top of the hill. The first house, that old rickety one, belonged to old man Svenson. Peggy and Maddie hurried past it, almost on tiptoe. Somebody said that once old man Svenson had shot a man. Others said, "Nonsense! He's an old good-for-nothing. Wouldn't hurt a flea."

But, false or true, the girls breathed more freely as they rounded the corner. It was too cold and drizzly for old man Svenson to be in his customary chair tilted against the house, chewing and spitting tobacco juice. Even his dog was nowhere in sight.

"I think that's where the Petronskis live," said Maddie, pointing to a little white house with lots of chicken coops on the side of it. Wisps of old grass stuck up here and there along the pathway like thin kittens. The house and its sparse little yard looked shabby but clean. It reminded Maddie of Wanda's one dress, her faded blue cotton dress, shabby but clean.

There was not a sign of life about the house. Peggy knocked firmly on the door, but there was no answer. She and Maddie went around to the back yard and knocked there. Still there was no answer.

"Wanda!" called Peggy. They listened sharply, but only a deep silence pressed against their ear drums. There was no doubt about it. The Petronskis were gone. How could they ever make amends?

They turned slowly and made their way back down the hill. It was a relief to be back on Oliver Street

again, but they still felt disconsolate, and Maddie wondered if she were going to be unhappy about Wanda
and the hundred dresses forever. Nothing would ever
seem good to her again because, just when she was
about to enjoy something — like going for a hike with
Peggy to look for bayberries, or sliding down Barley
Hill — she'd bump right smack into the thought that
she had made Wanda Petronski move away.

"Well, anyway," said Peggy. "She's gone now, so
what can we do? Besides, when I was asking her about
all her dresses, she probably was getting good ideas
for her drawings. She might not even have won the
contest, otherwise."

Maddie turned this idea carefully over in her head,
for if there were anything in it she would not have to
feel so badly. But that night she could not get to sleep.
She thought about Wanda and her faded blue house
dress and the little house she had lived in; and old
man Svenson living a few steps away. And she thought
of the glowing picture those hundred dresses made —
all lined up in the classroom.

At last Maddie sat up in bed and pressed her forehead tight in her hands and really thought. This was
the hardest thinking she had ever done. After a long,
long time, she reached an important conclusion.

She was never going to stand by and say nothing
again. If she ever heard anybody picking on some one
because they were funny looking, or because they had

strange names, she'd speak up. Even if it meant losing Peggy's friendship. She had no way of making things right with Wanda, but from now on she would never make anybody else that unhappy again. Finally, all tired out, Maddie fell asleep.

On Saturday Maddie spent the afternoon with Peggy. They were writing a letter to Wanda Petronski. It was just a friendly letter telling about the contest and telling Wanda she had won. They told her how pretty her drawings were and that now they were studying about Winfield Scott in school. And they asked her if she liked where she was living, and if she liked her new teacher. They had meant to say they were sorry, but it ended up with their just writing a friendly letter, the kind they would have written to any good friend, and they signed it with lots of X's for love. They mailed the letter to Boggins Heights, writing "Please Forward" on the envelope. The minute they dropped the letter in the mail box, they both felt happier and more carefree.

Days passed and there was no answer, but the letter did not come back, so maybe Wanda had received it. Perhaps she was so hurt and angry she was not going to answer. You could not blame her.

Weeks went by and still Wanda did not answer. Peggy had begun to forget the whole business, and Maddie put herself to sleep at night making speeches about Wanda, defending her from great crowds of

girls who were trying to tease her with, "How many
dresses have you got?" And before Wanda could press
her lips together in a tight line, the way she did before answering, Maddie would cry out, "Stop!" Then
everybody would feel ashamed the way she used to feel.

Now it was Christmas time and there was snow on
the ground. Christmas bells and a small tree decorated
the classroom. On the last day of school before the
holidays, the teacher showed the class a letter she had
received that morning.

"You remember Wanda Petronski, the gifted little
artist who won the drawing contest? Well, she has
written me, and I am glad to know where she lives,
because now I can send her her medal. And I hope
it gets there for Christmas. I want to read her letter
to you."

The class sat up with a sudden interest and listened
intently to Miss Mason as she read the letter.

Dear Miss Mason:

*How are you and Room Thirteen? Please tell the
girls they can keep those hundred dresses, because in my new house I have a hundred new
ones, all lined up in my closet. I'd like that girl
Peggy to have the drawing of the green dress with
the red trimmings, and her friend Maddie to have
the blue one. For Christmas. I miss that school*

and my new teacher does not equalize with you.
Merry Christmas to you and everybody.

Yours truly,
Wanda Petronski

On the way home from school Maddie and Peggy held their drawings very carefully. All the houses had wreaths and holly in the windows. Outside the grocery store, hundreds of Christmas trees were stacked, and in the window, candy peppermint sticks and cornucopias of shiny transparent paper were strung. The air smelled like Christmas and bright lights shining everywhere reflected different colors on the snow.

"Boy!" said Peggy, "this shows she really liked us. It shows she got our letter and this is her way of saying that everything's all right. And that's that," she said with finality.

"I hope so," said Maddie sadly. She felt sad because she knew she would never see the little tight-lipped Polish girl again and couldn't ever really make things right between them.

She went home and she pinned her drawing over a torn place in the pink-flowered wallpaper in the bedroom. The shabby room came alive from the brilliancy of the colors. Maddie sat down on the edge of her bed and looked at the drawing. She had stood by and said nothing, but Wanda had been nice to her, anyway.

Tears blurred her eyes and she gazed for a long time at the picture. Then hastily she rubbed her eyes and studied it intently. The colors in the dress were so vivid that she had scarcely noticed the face and head of the drawing. But it looked like her, Maddie! It really did. The same short blonde hair, blue eyes, and wide straight mouth. Why it really looked like her own self! Wanda had really drawn this for her. Excitedly, she ran over to Peggy's.

"Peg!" she said, "let me see your picture."

"What's the matter?" asked Peggy, as they clattered up the stairs to her room where Wanda's drawing was lying face down on the bed. Maddie carefully raised it.

"Look! She drew you. That's you!" she exclaimed. And the head and face of this picture did look like the auburn-haired Peggy.

"What did I say!" said Peggy. "She must have really liked us, anyway."

"Yes, she must have," agreed Maddie, and she blinked away the tears that came every time she thought of Wanda standing alone in that sunny spot in the schoolyard, looking stolidly over at the group of laughing girls, after she had walked off, after she had said, "Sure, a hundred of them, all lined up."